The Long Search

ZONDERVAN HEARTH BOOKS
Available from your Christian Bookseller

HEARTH BOOKS

HEARTH
BOOKS

A HEARTH MYSTERY

The Long Search

Sallie Lee Bell

ZONDERVAN
PUBLISHING HOUSE
OF THE ZONDERVAN CORPORATION | GRAND RAPIDS, MICHIGAN 49506

THE LONG SEARCH
Copyright 1958 by
Zondervan Publishing House
Grand Rapids, Michigan

First Zondervan Books edition   1974
Fifth printing   February 1978
ISBN 0-310-21012-7

Printed in the United States of America

CHAPTER 1

THE BUS ROLLED ALONG toward the east over the trackless miles of the Texas plains. As far as the eye could see, there was nothing but dry grass and tumbleweed that rolled lazily across the plain toward the cloudless horizon.

James Thornton gazed abstractedly out of the window at the uninteresting scene. Far in the distance there was a deer standing as still as if it were carved of stone, and presently an antelope came into view, walking slowly as if the heat had taken all of its speed and energy. They looked peaceful, he mused, even if the sun was hot enough to broil them. But then, they were used to the heat of summer as well as the biting winds of winter. A rabbit sped across the road ahead of them just in time to miss the wheels of the bus. Once safe from death, it squatted on its haunches and looked at the speeding bus. James smiled wryly. He could imagine that the rabbit cast an indignant look at the disappearing bus. "If he could speak, he'd probably bawl that driver out for upsetting his peaceful pursuit of food," the young man said under his breath.

He settled back into his seat and closed his eyes. The trip had been long and he was tired, but he couldn't sleep. One idea persisted in his troubled thoughts. He was on his way to kill a man. He opened his eyes with a start and looked about him as if he feared that the other passengers had read his thoughts. They were not even looking at him. They were as tired as he and most of them were either sleeping or reading. No one seemed to be talking.

It was a terrible thing to be on his way to commit murder. In spite of himself, he quailed before the word murder. But he had kept this determination in his heart for too long to let this brief dismay hinder him.

How long had it been since he had first determined to kill this man who had brought so much tragedy to his life? Ten years? Fifteen? No, not that long. Perhaps twelve — ever since he had been old enough to understand just what had happened to his father and to remember the name of the man who had been the cause of his death. It all seemed like a dream now, as he looked back on the past. The only reality was this grim determination to get revenge upon the one who had wrecked his life and his mother's life and had robbed him of all he would have known if his father had lived.

What would happen to him if he were caught after he had killed this heartless wretch? But he must not be caught. He must plan this revenge so that his victim would know why he was being killed. If he did not know, then half of the satisfaction of his revenge would be lost. He must plan it so that after the deed was done he could get away before the crime was detected. He did not want to die even though it seemed that life had little prospect of joy for him. He was young and in time, after the grief over his mother's death had lessened, perhaps he could find happiness, the happiness to which he was entitled.

He remembered the first time he had mentioned his determination to kill this man. He was a little fellow, too little really to understand just what had happened. His mother had told him a part of the truth about his father's death. He had worried her so persistently to know where his father was and why he did not come home for such a long time — for he had idolized his father — that she was forced to tell him he was in prison. He remembered how she had cried after she had told him and he could still feel the chill that stole over him when he realized the truth. Young as he was, he knew the stigma attached to the family of a prisoner.

He realized later why some of the children in the neighborhood had refused to play with him. They had shunned him and he had been too proud to ask why. In his childish heart there was a great ache, for he missed his father terribly. They had been pals and his father had had many plans for his only child. Though James couldn't understand all of them, he was enthused just because his father seemed enthused while he was telling them.

He had said that they would travel to far places. James would go to the best school in the state and during every vacation they would travel. The thought of train rides and boat rides intrigued him as a child, even though those far places were vague, shadowy regions. His world was no larger than his yard and the stores downtown. He remembered how his mother had sat nearby listening with a smile on her face, a smile of indulgence for the husband she adored, even though she knew that perhaps all of these dreams might not be realized. They were not wealthy, but James Thornton, Sr., was in a business which gave promise of wealth.

Then had come tragedy. James Thornton had been accused of murder. The business which had given such promise of wealth had been robbed consistently by one of the employees. Another had discovered the theft and had been murdered by the man who had been stealing from the firm. The man accused was James Thornton. The only one who could have saved him was his partner, Thomas Martin. Instead of witnessing for the defense, Martin had been the main witness for the prosecution. He had testified that he had caught Thornton in the act of destroying incriminating papers and had afterwards found the body of the man Thornton was accused of killing. Thornton was sentenced to life imprisonment.

James had known nothing of the facts until he had grown to manhood. He had never been allowed to see his father. He had held that against his mother until she had told him after his father's death that this was his father's wish. He did not want his son to see him behind prison bars.

When he was older he could realize what his mother had suffered and how she grieved, though she never said a word to him. She tried to make his life happy and help him forget that his father was a condemned criminal.

He remembered her visits to the prison when he was still little. She would leave him with one of her neighbors, one of her few sympathetic friends. When she returned he could see the stark misery of her eyes and her pale face, even though she would greet him with a smile and a cheerful word.

Finally his father died in prison. He was old enough by then to be told that his father had died and that he would be buried far from home. There was not enough money to bring the body home. James had heard his mother sobbing in a burst of grief and saying, "He was murdered, just as surely as if he had been shot by Tom Martin. Someday I hope that he suffers as much as he has made us suffer."

James had begged her to tell him what she meant by those words and when he would not be put off any longer, she had told him a part of the truth. It was then that he had clenched his fist and cried out that he would kill the man who had wronged his father.

His mother had put her arms around him and had told him that he must never think of doing a thing like that, for two wrongs never made a right. He had never repeated his threat, but he had kept that determination in his heart. He would find that man if it took the rest of his life and he would make him suffer as he had made them suffer, then he would kill him. He had pictured in his childish imagination a number of fiendish schemes for torturing Martin. Then he would tell him why he was torturing him. After that he would kill him. After that — he had no answer.

This grim determination had festered in his heart with the hate that grew with the passing years until it became an obsession. He never mentioned this to his mother but she often wondered why the boy who had been such a happy child grew into a glum, embittered young man. It worried her and she did everything she could to change him and bring the sunshine back into his nature, but it seemed impossible. Then her health failed. The long years of heartache and the struggle to keep them going had been too mucn for her frail strength. Finally she died and James was left alone.

He was now free to hunt for Thomas Martin and to fulfill his plan for revenge. But now that he was on his way to seek the man he wondered why he had kept this hate in his heart all these years. It had warped his whole life, but he was not conscious of that as he sat remembering all the wasted years of his father's life, all the grief-laden years that filled his mother's life and all his own lost opportunities. He thought of those plans of his father's for their vacation trips. The only trip his father had ever taken was to the penitentiary — sent there by the man who had actually committed the crime. Whenever this thought came to James hate and the determination for revenge rose within him with renewed force and he had no thought of consequences, only the grim, dogged determination to make this man suffer as he had made others suffer.

The bus rumbled on over the parched plains while he sat with eyes closed, lost in the dark world of his hate until finally the bus came to a stop and he opened his eyes to see who was departing or boarding the bus. He hoped that no one would occupy the seat next to him. He wanted to be alone. He had been alone for so long, it seemed, that he did not feel the need of any human companionship. Even his mother had seemed outside of his life at times, though he grieved deeply when she had died.

He could still see her now as she was the last time he had looked upon her face. She was cold and still as she lay in her casket, but there was a look of peace upon her face that he had not seen there since his father had been taken to prison. The deep lines of worry and sorrow had etched themselves upon her once lovely face, but now as she lay with hands folded quietly, those lines had been erased by the cold hand of death. She was finally at rest after the long years of anxiety and struggle and grief. He could not remember when those hands had been at rest before. They had always been busy, either sewing for her few customers or working about the house and trying to amuse him.

His memories of the past were interrupted as a passenger entered the bus and searched for a seat. She was a young thing, surely not more than twenty, and the suitcase which she carried seemed too heavy for her. James saw that she had noticed the seat next to him and she struggled down the narrow aisle while her bag bumped against every seat. He wondered why the driver had not put the bag in the baggage compartment, but he had not noticed that she refused to be parted from it. The driver had allowed her to carry it inside the bus.

She stopped by the empty seat and hesitated, then said timidly,

"Would you mind if I sit here?"

He shook his head and motioned for her to sit down. He did mind, but he couldn't tell her so and she had a right to sit there. She looked at the space above the seat and her face clouded with distress, then she turned to him appealingly.

"I'm afraid I can't lift my bag that high. Would you mind putting it up for me?"

He got up silently and put the bag in the rack above, then sat down again without saying a word or looking at her. It was rather ungracious of him, he knew, but he did not feel like talking. And he did not want to be bothered by a helpless female. He had a problem to work out and he did not want to be disturbed in his moody thinking, his heart-breaking memories and his desire for revenge. Now that he was on his quest to carry out that revenge, his soul recoiled at the prospect and it made him angry with himself that he should feel this sudden reluctance after harboring a dream of vengeance for so many years.

He kept his eyes fixed upon the scene outside, though it was monotonous and unchanging across the barren plains. He did not even steal a glance at the girl beside him, for he felt that she was looking at him. She had settled herself in her seat after a murmured thanks when he had put her bag in the rack above. He felt guilty for being so boorish, but he would not yield to the urge to be polite. His mother had done her best to make him the kind of boy that his father would have had him be and, except for this secret hate which he carried like a hidden viper within him, he had been all that she could have desired.

When at last he turned for a swift glance at the girl, he saw that she was asleep. She had removed her hat, and her head was resting against the back of the seat as relaxed as that of a child. He took time for a closer inspection and his heart twisted with sudden pain. How much like his mother she looked as she sat there with eyes closed, calm and relaxed! She was as fragile as his mother had been. Her pale gold hair was much lighter than his mother's and of course she was much younger, younger than he could remember his mother ever having been. He remembered how his mother had seemed to fade like a delicate flower whose roots had been brutally torn from their moorings, until she had wilted and had finally given up the struggle to go on living. The comparison startled him. This girl seemed like her, as if she, too, had had her roots torn from their safe moorings and had almost given up the struggle to go on, even though she was young. He felt suddenly sorry for her. He wondered if she had known even a little of the pain that his mother had known. He hoped that she had not. She was lovely and life could hold much for her. Her skin was so white that it seemed almost transparent and her small hands that lay quietly upon her lap seemed too fragile for any kind of work. What was she doing on this bus, he wondered, and where was she going?

He laughed silently at his own foolish thoughts, then the laugh was suddenly silenced, for two great teardrops slipped from under her long lashes and trickled down her pale cheeks. As if she felt his gaze fixed upon her, she suddenly opened her gray eyes wide and caught him staring at her. She gave a startled gasp and wiped the tears from her eyes with a childish gesture as she sat erect. Color flooded her face.

"I must have fallen asleep," she said with a note of surprise.

"It will do you good to get some sleep," he told her, trying to cover his embarrassment at being caught staring. "If you have a long way to go, you should sleep all you can. This scenery isn't worth wasting your eyesight on."

"I'm going to New Orleans," she told him. "It's a long way, isn't it?"

"Yes, we won't be there until tomorrow noon."

"Are you going that far?" she asked hopefully.

"Yes, that's where I'm going."

He wasn't pleased to know that he would have her with him all the way. He wanted to be alone and she had evoked too many painful memories.

"Oh, that will be nice." She gave him a smile, then her face colored again. "I — I — mean it will be nice to have someone to talk to. All these other passengers seem to have someone with them."

He did not reply and her face clouded. She turned and looked out the window on the other side of the bus.

He felt sudden pity for her. She seemed almost a child, though he knew that she was older than she seemed. There was something pathetic about her so he made an effort to be agreeable.

"Are you going to visit someone in New Orleans?" he asked.

"I'm going to live with my aunt. My mother died a short time ago and I have no one else."

She turned away to hide the tears which he knew were filling her eyes. They were beautiful eyes, large and deep gray, with long lashes that curved upward, adding to her little-girl appearance.

"I'm sorry," he volunteered, wishing that he could say something to stop those tears. "I know just how you feel. I lost my mother recently, too." His heart ached in tune with hers. He knew what she suffered.

She turned back to him with tears still on her lashes.

"Then you really do understand, don't you?" Her voice

12

choked with suppressed sobs while she tried to smile. "I hate to be such a baby, but my mother and I were so close and I miss her. It doesn't seem worthwhile to go on without her, but I guess we have to go on whether we want to or not."

"Yes, we do," he agreed. "Life may never seem the same to you, but you are so young that in time you will get over the keenness of your grief and you will be happy again."

"Is that the way you feel?" she asked hopefully. "I don't seem to want to face the future without her."

"I haven't had time to think about myself or what life may hold for me," he said as the cloud of his obsession settled upon him again.

After he had accomplished his mission, what would life hold for him? Prison? Execution? Flight from the law? Constant fear of pursuit and capture? He refused to think what would happen afterwards. First let him find the man he sought, then he could begin to think of the consequences and plan for what might happen.

"But you're pretty young yourself," she offered with a smile. "Life can still hold the same for you that you say it can hold for me." The tears had been wiped away and she was in command of her emotions once more. "Mother used to say that for one who loved the Lord, the best was always ahead."

He turned surprised eyes upon her. "Your mother must have been a religious person to say something like that."

He had never heard his mother make a statement like that. In fact, he had never heard her say much about God, even though she was sweet and gentle and uncomplaining.

"My mother was a Christian," she replied. A look of sadness shadowed her expressive face. "She often talked to me about being one, but I was never interested and I am sure that I must have grieved her by my indifference." She uttered a sigh, so deep and so profound that it seemed to reach his own deep sorrow. "The last words she said to me I'll never forget. She said, 'I'm going home, darling. I shall be looking for you. Promise me that you will follow on to know the Lord.'" Once more she fought back the tears.

"Did you promise?" He was interested in spite of himself. He no longer resented her presence and he had forgotten his desire to be alone.

She shook her head. "Somehow I couldn't, because I felt that I wouldn't be telling the truth. I didn't have any desire to live as she did. She told me one day that I should be careful not to turn the Lord away, for I might turn Him away for the last time and then I would never have another opportunity to accept salvation. While she was waiting for me to promise her what she asked, she just closed her eyes and left me. That's what hurts so, that I didn't promise."

"It's just as well you didn't make a promise that you didn't want to keep," he offered, trying to comfort her. "Sometimes people ask impossible things on their deathbeds and it isn't fair to those who are left."

"But I should have given her that promise. It is something that I should try to keep, but I just don't feel any desire to keep it."

He had no answer and a silence fell between them.

"Wouldn't you rather sit by the window?" he asked presently.

"No. I'm all right here. I don't really care to look out. I'd rather rest and try to forget."

"Try to go to sleep," he advised. "That will help."

She smiled and laid her head against the seat and closed her eyes.

He looked at her again as her eyes remained closed and he resented the sympathy he had for her. He did not want to be interested in anyone. He had a sinister task to perform and there must be no room for sympathy or interest in anyone until that task was completed. He turned his gaze once more to the seared plains. How he wished that he could forget! But he had nursed this scheme of vengeance too long. It had grown until it had become a monster within him, controlling his every thought and coloring every purpose that he might have had in his past life, and now taking hold of his whole future. Where it would end he did not know and, just now, he did not care.

CHAPTER 2

THE BUS STOPPED and the passengers piled out for dinner, glad of the opportunity to walk about and break the monotony of the ride. Texas might be a wonderful state, James said to himself, but the beauty of it must be somewhere off in the far spaces. He had not encountered any of it on this trip.

He rose and stretched himself, then turned to see if the girl was still asleep. She had sat quietly for so long that he was sure she must have been sleeping, but when he stood she opened her eyes and looked inquiringly at him.

"We're stopping to eat," he told her. "You'd better go and get something. The night will be long and you'll get hungry."

She rose and stood in the aisle while he went ahead, then she followed. He had not asked her to accompany him, but she followed him nevertheless and sat down opposite him at the only unoccupied table.

"Do you mind if I sit here?" she asked.

"Of course not." He managed a smile. "What will you have?" he asked as he looked over the menu.

"I think I'll just take a doughnut and coffee."

He thought she was ordering this because she did not have money for a full meal and again he felt sorry for her. The shadows under her eyes told of sleepless nights and of grief. He could understand what she had experienced, for the memory of his own experience was fresh and the poignancy of his grief was still there, though he had tried to bury it when he started on his search.

"You'd better eat more than that," he advised. "We won't stop again until morning for breakfast. I'm going to order a good thick steak. That will be enough for both of us. How about some fried potatoes and a salad?" He felt that he was being extravagant, for he did not have much money himself, but she reminded him of a little lost kitten and he wanted to see her eat a good meal and enjoy it.

"I couldn't let you do that," she demurred. "I could order the potatoes and the salad and share them with you."

"You can order something for breakfast, but let me do this now. The order will be more than I can eat and there's no use letting good food go to waste."

He gave the order without further comment and as they waited for it to be filled, they sat silent for a time looking at the other passengers.

"I wonder what they find to talk about," he remarked. "Some people always seems to be talking, but they never seem to say anything worthwhile."

"I've always wished that I could talk easily." She smiled ruefully. "Mother used to say that sometimes silence is golden, but I'm afraid that's not the truth with me. It's just plain stupid."

"That remark wasn't stupid. In fact, it sounded wise." He gave her a smile that was a little more friendly. She was not only a little lost kitten, she was a lovely girl, as fragile as a costly bit of china, with delicate coloring and features that would grace a miniature.

His interest in her and his admiration of her beauty were purely impersonal. No thought of romance entered his mind. He had no time for romance. Romance and murder would not mix. The thought of what he planned to do brought another feeling of revulsion, but he grimly tried to conquer this unpleasant sensation as their order came and they began to eat. She protested as he piled her plate with potatoes and gave her half of the steak, but he only smiled as he set the plate before her.

"You look as if you need a few thick steaks. They would put a few pounds on you and bring back the color to your cheeks."

"I haven't felt like eating for a long time," she said while her eyes clouded. "While Mother was sick I was anxious about her, then when she died, I just couldn't eat. I really am enjoying this," she added brightly. "This steak must have come from some of our good Texas beef."

"I suppose those uninteresting plains are good for something after all," he remarked. "They look like a lot of waste land to me."

"Without them there would be no good cattle grazing grounds and people would be wishing for steaks that they'd never get."

"Now I call that saying the right words at the right time and spoken like a Texan," he said.

She laughed. He observed how her face became alight and animated when she laughed. He thought that perhaps this was the first time she had laughed in quite some time.

"I didn't know that I could do it," she remarked with a twinkle in her deep gray eyes.

"Have you ever been to New Orleans?" he asked.

"No. My aunt moved there after my father died and then Mother and I couldn't afford to visit her. Mother worked until she got sick and I worked after I finished school. I do hope my aunt will be there to meet me as she said she would. I'd feel lost in that city if she weren't there."

"I'm sure she will be if she said she would."

He was hoping she would be there. He didn't want this girl on his hands when he reached New Orleans. He had his own affairs to attend to. The little lost kitten would be a nuisance if her aunt didn't appear.

"Have you ever been to New Orleans?" she asked.

"No. I've lived in the west all of my life."

"Are you going there for a visit or just on business?"

"I'm going on business."

He could feel the sudden gravity in his voice and he could feel the grimness of that business once more enveloping him with its sinister hold. He wished he could forget it, but its hold upon him was too strong.

She noticed the sudden change, the shadow in his eyes, the grim lines about his mouth and she wondered about it.

"I hope everything will work out all right for you," she said. "You have helped to make this trip pleasant when I was dreading it so much."

"I'm glad if I helped," he replied.

She hoped that his business would work out all right! If she only knew what that business was she would shun him as if he had the plague. If it did work out all right he would never see her again, that was certain. He would be on his way, fleeing from the law. All the rest of his life he would be fleeing even if no one pursued him. He would be fleeing from his own guilty conscience, and from that there would be no escape. But he would have paid the debt and just now that was all that mattered. Somewhere in New Orleans there was a man who must suffer as he had made his father suffer. Not in the same way. That would be too good for him. Long years in prison, even in mental anguish would be far too good. He would still be alive. He must make him suffer both physical as well as mental anguish before he died. First he must find that man. That might take time and he was anxious to begin his search as soon as he had reached the city.

"You must be thinking about your mother," she ventured timidly as she saw the dark look upon his face.

He covered himself with an effort. "I was thinking about that business of mine," he told her truthfully. "But that can wait. Let's have some ice cream to top off this meal."

When they returned to the bus they talked for a while, then they settled back for the long night ride. Presently the lights were turned out and all was silent, but James could not sleep. Once during the night the bus stopped to let a passenger leave. He opened his eyes and looked about him and saw that the girl was also awake. She gave him a faint smile.

"I can't sleep very well. I'm not used to this noise," she said.

"Neither am I. You never did tell me your name," he remarked.

"It's Faith. Faith Ransom."

"Faith Ransom," he repeated. "That's pretty."

"Mother said it was typical. She said that Ransom was what Jesus did when He shed His blood for our sins and that we have to accept the gift of eternal life through faith, so when she married Daddy and I came along, she said that Faith fitted so well with Ransom that she could not name me anything else. I'm sure that I disappointed her when I never did have the faith she hoped and prayed that I would have."

"Perhaps someday you will."

His words carried no conviction to himself, for he knew nothing of the faith she mentioned, but he had to say something, for sadness had overshadowed her again.

"I do want to feel that I shall see her again. She used to say that God would answer the prayer of faith and then she would smile and say that that meant me." She was silent a moment, then she said, "You never did tell me your name."

"I'm James Thornton."

"My father's name was James. Mother used to call him Jimmie. He never would let anyone else call him that. Said it sounded too silly, as if he were just a kid. Mother used to tell him that he was just like a little boy to her. I'll always love that name."

There was no coquetry in her eyes as they looked into his. She was not really thinking of him, he knew, but of her father and mother who were gone. The lights went out and the bus got under way again and they continued the long night ride in silence. Finally they both slept and did not stir until the first rays of the sun shone through the window across their faces.

They had entered Louisiana and the scene had changed. Instead of sun-scorched plains there were willows and moss-covered oaks, sluggish bayous, fields of rice and vast fields of tall cotton.

They passed along the borders of plantations where sugar cane grew high, with the long, slender leaves waving gently in the early morning breeze. It was cooler along the way, for they were not too far from the Gulf. The passengers who boarded the bus spoke in the peculiar Cajun dialect that was English with a foreign accent and an occasional French word thrown in unconsciously. Many of these South Louisiana people spoke only Cajun. They chattered volubly and loudly as the bus sped on toward New Orleans.

The traffic increased as they neared the city and the highway widened, giving them the opportunity for better speed. Motels with swimming pools in small courtyards dotted the highway, and then they passed under the approach to the Mississippi River Bridge.

Faith watched the scene eagerly and with growing excitement as the bus crossed one of the overpasses and turned down Canal Street. They looked out the front of the bus and the wide street with its neutral ground in the middle stretched before them as far as they could see, toward the river which was hidden from view by docks and the ferry landing.

"It's beautiful!" she exclaimed.

"I don't think there is another street like it in America," James remarked.

The bus turned in at the station and the passengers began getting their possessions together and crowding into the aisle, eager to get out. James got her bag down and offered to carry it out for her.

"Thanks again for being so kind to me," she said as they followed the others outside. "Perhaps we shall meet again. If we don't, I want to wish you success in your business and in everything that life can bring you."

"Thanks," he replied. "And may you soon be happy again."

Success in his business! Again the cloud descended over him. If she only knew what would be involved if her wish should come true!

CHAPTER 3

JAMES WAITED IMPATIENTLY for his baggage to be delivered and he forgot about the girl and the aunt who was supposed to meet her. He was impatient to get out and look for a place to stay. While he looked over the thinning line of passengers leaving the depot, he saw her standing there, bewildered and forlorn, looking anxiously about her.

He picked up his bags and started to leave when she called to him.

"Oh, please wait a minute!" she cried, hurrying to where he stood.

He put his bags down and waited impatiently for her.

"My aunt isn't here," she said in distress. "I wonder what happened. What shall I do?"

He could not fail to be touched by her distress. He saw that she was on the verge of tears. He sighed. He had that little lost kitten on his hands again and he couldn't refuse to offer his help.

"Does your aunt have a phone?" he asked.

"Yes, I didn't think of that. I have her address and phone number here in my purse."

"Let's go inside and call," he suggested.

He led the way inside, then he put his bags in a storage

compartment and went to a telephone booth to call the aunt's number. He let the phone ring several times but there was no answer.

"She doesn't seem to be home," he told her. "We'll wait here a little while and see if she comes for you. She may have been delayed. If she doesn't come, we'll take a taxi and go out to her house."

"I hope she isn't sick," Faith murmured.

They sat silently for a while, and as James fumed inwardly Faith waited anxiously, too worried to try to talk. When at last he was sure that the woman was not coming, he went outside and hailed a taxi. He put her bag inside and they rode to the address of the aunt. She lived far downtown and the drive was long.

"I hate to put you to this much trouble," Faith remarked. "I'm taking up too much of your time."

"Forget it," he said, none too graciously.

When they finally reached the house he told the driver to wait for him. He rang the bell and waited impatiently for someone to answer. After repeated ringing he knew no one was there. He was wondering what he should do next, when a woman living next door stuck her head outside and asked them what they wanted.

"We're looking for Mrs. Mary Hamilton," James told her.

"Oh, my!" the woman ejaculated. "Don't you know what happened to her?"

"No," James replied as a foreboding of disaster took possession of him. "We just came in on the bus this morning. She is this young lady's aunt."

"Dear me!" the woman said, coming out and joining them. "Mrs. Hamilton was buried yesterday."

"Oh!" It was a horrified cry from Faith. She swayed and turned so white James feared that she would faint. He put an arm around her to steady her and he could feel her small body trembling.

"Mrs. Hamilton had a heart attack and she was dead when we found her. I went in to take the paper since she

22

always let me read it after she had finished, and there she was, out cold. The doctor said she had been dead for a couple of hours, perhaps. We didn't know she had any relatives, so she was buried the next day. I'm sorry, Miss, that I didn't know about you."

Faith's stricken face touched his heart even though he had been chagrined at the delay she had caused. She looked at him appealingly.

"What shall I do?" she asked as the tears ran down her cheeks. "I don't have anyone else in the world."

"You could stay here in your aunt's house," the woman suggested. "I have the key. The court was waiting to see what should be done about the furniture and everything."

"I couldn't stay here," Faith moaned. "I just couldn't. I don't know what to do."

"I'll find a place for you tonight and tomorrow we'll see what can be done," James said. He turned to the neighbor. "If anyone comes to do anything about the house, tell them that the niece is here and will look after everything."

They got into the taxi and drove back to the depot. Once inside the taxi Faith gave way to tears and sobbed quietly.

"Don't take it too hard, little one," he said soothingly as he laid a hand upon her arm. "Everything will turn out all right, I'm sure. Just buck up and try to be brave."

"How can I when I don't have anyone else in the world and I have so little money?"

"You have me and I'll do all I can to get you settled. I'll help you look after everything. It may take time to get your aunt's affairs straightened out, but perhaps you will have enough to tide you over until you can get adjusted and find something to do. You're still young and you have all of life before you. Don't despair. Everything will work out all right, I'm sure."

He felt that his long speech was empty of real comfort, for he couldn't feel that he was giving her any, but she turned to him with a slight smile.

"You're good to me when I've been such a nuisance.

23

How I thank you for being so kind! What would I have done if I hadn't had you?''

He wondered just what she would have done and in spite of his impatience to be on his own he was glad that he had been there when she needed someone.

Back at the depot, he got a newspaper and looked over the want ads to find a room. Finally he found one that seemed to be what he was looking for and they set out to find it. It proved to be more attractive than he had hoped.

It was in the old Garden District in the upper part of the city. The house was old, but the rooms were clean and large and there were two available. The price was reasonable and he decided that he might as well take the other for himself until he could decide just what he would do. It would be easier for him to help the girl. He was hoping that it would not take too long to get her affairs straightened out.

The landlady, Mrs. Thomas, was sympathetic when James told her about Faith's tragedy, and seemed eager to help them.

''When you've unpacked your bag and rested for a while, we'll go out and get something to eat,'' he told Faith. Then he turned to go to his own room.

''Thanks for everything,'' Faith said as she closed the door and he followed Mrs. Thomas down the hall.

''Poor little thing,'' Mrs. Thomas remarked. ''Have you known her long?''

''I only met her on the bus,'' James explained. Then he told her how they had met and how helpless she was when her aunt had not appeared at the depot to meet her.

He unpacked his bags, then lay down and tried to rest, but he could not. He got up and paced the floor as he tried to plan what he should do. First he would study the telephone book, then he would contact every Thomas Martin listed there. If he did not find the man this way, he would search the city directory. If he failed to find the man in either book, he would be at a loss to know what to do next. He set his lips firmly as he vowed again that if it took the rest of his life he would spend it looking for this man. If he had changed his name, that would prove a problem, but he would not face that fact until he had failed to find him under his real name.

It was almost dusk when he knocked at Faith's door. She opened it at once and he saw that she was ready to go with him. She looked rested and he was glad for that.

"You look so fresh and rested that you must have had some sleep," he remarked as they went down the hall together.

"I did sleep some," she said. "I was glad, for when I was asleep I couldn't think and thinking frightens me."

"Don't let it frighten you," he advised. "I'm sure that everything will work out all right."

"You're a comfort," she sighed. "What would I do without you?"

A warm glow spread through him at her words. It was good to feel that he was being helpful. He forgot his impatience to be rid of her. They inquired of Mrs. Thomas and she directed them to a little restaurant not far away. The evening had cooled and it was pleasant on the street. They passed lovely old homes of another generation on Prytania Street, houses with wide porches and broad steps, houses that sat back from the street behind high iron fences, shaded by ancient oaks, with bricked walks winding through old-fashioned gardens where shrubs and flowers grew in profusion. An air of refinement pervaded the atmosphere of these old homes, though many of them had been converted into rooming houses and some of them bore the marks of neglect and decay.

"This city is different from any place I've ever seen before," she remarked as they walked along, interested in the scene. "Everything seems old yet attractive."

"This is an old city, one of the oldest in this part of the country," he replied. "It is quite different from the new towns which have sprung up suddenly in your State of Texas. This old city has a part of France in it along with the newer English section, yet the old-world atmosphere mellows it all and makes it different from any other city. That's why people flock here all through the year and enjoy the things that make it different.''

''You talk as if you were a native,'' she remarked.

''I've read a lot about it,'' he replied.

He did not tell her why he had read so much about it. It had long been the center of his thought.

''I must pay for my meal,'' she insisted as they gave their order. ''You have already spent too much on me. I'm sure my money will hold out until I can get a job.''

''If you insist,'' he said. He knew that she would feel better if he let her feel more independent. ''I'm sure that you will be able to get something from your aunt's furniture and whatever else she may have left, if there are no other relatives.''

''There is no one but me,'' she told him. ''I'm sure she didn't have much money.''

''Whatever it is, it will help you until you can get adjusted and get some kind of a job.''

''I want to begin work as soon as I can. I shall be better satisfied if I'm occupied. I'd die, just sitting in that room with no one to talk to.''

''You'll soon make friends. Just try to believe that the best is yet ahead.''

''You're a great comfort.'' She gave him a bright smile. ''I feel better already.''

He wished he could say the same for himself.

CHAPTER 4

THE NEXT DAY James took Faith to attend to her aunt's affairs. They took the bus to Canal Street and then walked down Royal to the court building. She was interested in the quaint old French Quarter as they walked down the street where antique shops displayed numerous wares in the windows and for the present she forgot her grief and her worry over the future.

She stopped and scanned the displays of antiques with wide eyes and smothered exclamations of delight and she begged James to go inside with her in one or two of the shops so that she could see the furniture and ornaments crowded in them. The prices seemed enormously high. She loved beautiful things and she had never seen such an array of antiques before. She did not know, of course, that many of the pieces displayed as antiques were manufactured in the rear of some of the stores or upstairs above them.

"If I ever have a home, I hope that I can have some of these lovely things in it," she remarked as they came out on the street again. "We never had anything very beautiful in our home and everything in the stores back home was new and different."

"These lovely old things that are so high priced were no

27

doubt bought for a song from old French families who lost their wealth,'' he said. ''I'm sure that they were priceless in the eyes of those who once owned them.''

''You must have done a lot of reading,'' she observed, ''about New Orleans. Why were you so interested in the city if you've never been here?''

''I've always wanted to come here,'' he said guardedly, ''but while my mother was living I never had the chance. It has held my interest ever since I was a little fellow. I see it holds yours now.''

She smiled. ''Yes, it does. I suppose everyone who comes here for the first time is struck by its difference from other cities. Some of the sections we have seen have been drab and others are modern and attractive.''

They passed doorways where she could get a glimpse of paved brick courtyards where banana plants grew, their thick, fringed leaves drooping over small fountains. She paused in the entry of one and saw the winding stairway in the rear that led to the narrow porch with green blinds enclosing the rooms above.

''It must be interesting to live in these apartments,'' she said as they returned to the street once more, ''but I don't think I'd like staying in them. Somehow they make me think of mice and lizards and other creeping things. The bricks are moldy and those rooms look as if the sun never really gets to them.''

''Perhaps you're right about the creeping things in some of the houses in this section,'' he said. ''Some of these places look as if they had not been cleaned in ages. Let's do the rest of the sightseeing when we have finished our business. It's time for us to be there now.''

They did not have far to go before they came to the court building, an attractive edifice with white columns and wide steps leading to the entrance. They were sent from one office to another before they found the right place. The clerk in charge of the records told them that Faith would have to establish her identity and prove that she was her aunt's only heir before she could receive whatever property or money her aunt might have left. This would take time and James inwardly fumed at the delay. Since he had undertaken to help her, he would have to carry on until her claim was settled. He felt that she would get little from the household effects, but even that would help until she could get a position of some kind. He decided that when her affairs were finally settled he would get a room somewhere else so that he would not be bothered any further.

When they had finished at the courthouse, she asked if he would walk with her through the Vieux Carre and since he could do nothing with his own plans for the day, he agreed.

He was amused by her childish delight in the unusual sights of the old section of the city and he had to admit that he was enjoying the trip more than he had anticipated. The lure of the city was interesting him in spite of himself.

They walked through Jackson Square, the old parade ground, known as the Place D'Armes, where three flags had waved from the flagpole in the center of the square. The figure of General Andrew Jackson now occupied the central spot in the square.

"He was the hero of the Battle of New Orleans," he told her. "He won the battle against the British, in spite of their far superior forces. Hundreds of British were slain in one of the bloodiest battles of the War of 1812. The Pirate Jean Lafitte and his men did much to help in that battle. The terrible part of it was that the battle was so unnecessary. The treaty of peace had already been signed before the battle was fought. If news could have traveled as fast in those days as it does now, hundreds of those British soldiers would have been alive to go back to their families."

"All war is horrible and unnecessary," she said as they stood below the statue. "Mother said that if men and nations could only realize that war never really decided anything, perhaps they would not be so ready to fight. She used to tell me when I was a little girl that one day when Jesus returned to this earth to reign, there would be no more wars, that there would be peace and happiness for all the earth and that there would be no more sickness and no more sorrow."

"That would be something," he replied. "Sounds too good to be true."

He was not particularly interested in the stories her mother had told her. He was wondering how long it would take to get her affairs settled. He wondered where this Thomas Martin lived and what kind of life he had lived since he had ended his business in the west and returned to the city of his birth.

"I used to pretend all sorts of things that I would do when the Lord Jesus came back on earth to reign," she continued, not noticing his silence. "Mother said that those who had been true to Him in this life would go on through eternity to a greater happiness than anyone could imagine."

"Sounds like a fairy tale," he commented.

"To me it was more interesting than any fairy tale I ever heard. Mother seemed glad because I always wanted to hear more. She was hoping that I would want to become a Christian when I grew older, but instead, I lost interest in what she had tried to teach me about the Bible. I disliked going to church, but I went just to please her. I wish I could be different, but I just don't want to be."

"Perhaps you will someday when you are older," he offered as they left the square and went into the old Cabildo which was once a government house.

"I doubt it. I don't have any desire to be different. I guess that perhaps God will have to deal with me before I have any sense at all about spiritual things. He'll have to knock some sense into my head," she added childishly.

"It has to do with the heart more than the head, doesn't it?" he asked with a wisdom of which he was not aware.

"You're right," she replied with a smile, then she turned her attention to the scene around them. "I've been rambling on and boring you. I don't know why I did that. I wonder what this room is."

They had mounted the wide stairway, worn by the footsteps of generations and entered the room just beyond the landing. They discovered that this was the room where the purchase of Louisiana, the territory which occupied such a vast area of present-day United States, was finally concluded when the papers were signed. They looked with interest at the paintings on the wall of Napoleon and the other notables who were in positions of power at the time of the purchase.

As they wandered through the many rooms and finally went out into the courtyard, James became more interested. He was seeing things about which he had read and studied when he was just a child. His interest had dated from the time when his mother had revealed to him that Thomas Martin had lived here and had come back here after the trial and imprisonment of his father. It was not long after the conclusion of the trial that the business had been sold and Martin had left. James tried not to think of Martin as they wandered through the courtyard. He was enjoying this trip far more than he had anticipated. He had been reluctant to waste any more time on sightseeing, but he enjoyed Faith's enthusiasm and her interest in everything she saw. She asked him about everything as if he were a guide and he laughingly remarked that he was not really a bureau of information.

"You know enough to be one," she replied. "What you don't know, just make up. I won't know the difference and if I ask too many questions, just tell me when to be quiet. I don't want to be a nuisance."

"You're not," he assured her. "I'm getting a double enjoyment from this. I'm enjoying the sights myself and I'm getting a big kick out of seeing how much you enjoy them."

"I'm going to like this wonderful city," she remarked as they crossed the courtyard.

"This is where slaves were kept who had committed some crime," he told her as they entered one of the small rooms. The heavy door had a small iron grill at the top and behind this room there was another one with no opening except the grill at the top of the door.

"This must have been the dungeon where the worst ones were kept in solitary. This must have been the jail where all criminals were kept," he amended as they looked around. "I believe that when the British were approaching the city and every man was needed to defend it, the prisoners were given their freedom and were armed to march with the others to the battlefield down at Chalmette. After the battle they were given a pardon. There were not too many Americans killed, but the British were slaughtered by hundreds."

"Did you make a specialty of New Orleans history?" she asked. "I can't imagine you knowing so much about the city since you've never been here before."

"History was my favorite study at school and I was much interested in the history of Louisiana, especially New Orleans."

It was time for lunch and when they stopped in front of the Patio Royal he suggested that they have lunch there. The interior was quaint and typical of old New Orleans. They saw the vault under the stairs which had once been a part of the old bank and they wandered into the lovely courtyard where tables were placed under large umbrellas. Large shrubs and banana plants grew in profusion around the high walls enclosing the patio and fragrant annuals bordered the beds.

Almost every table was occupied, for this was a favorite eating place for citizens as well as tourists. The prices were astonishingly high, but James insisted that he should pay for the meal and that they would forget finances for this one day. The food was excellent and they enjoyed the well-seasoned French cooking, especially the shrimp salad with a pungent dressing that brought tears to Faith's eyes, but which she ate with relish, nevertheless.

"This coffee is black as ink," she said as the beverage was served. "It surely isn't like the coffee we had at home."

"No. But I like it," he said. "I can understand why people who live here have a hard time drinking the coffee we are used to. It must taste like weak tea."

When they finally returned to their rooming house Faith was tired and felt that she should rest.

"I'll say it again," she told him as they stopped at her door. "How can I ever thank you for what you have done for me? What would I have done if I had not sat beside you on the bus? I shall be grateful all the rest of my life."

"I'm glad I was there." He gave her a smile. "I've

enjoyed the day as much as you have."

"Mother would have said that this was all in the plan of God, my meeting you. She always said that everything would work out for my good if I would only love the Lord. It surely has worked out for my good since I met you."

He was touched and embarrassed by her words.

"Get a nap and have a good rest," he said. "I think I shall get some sleep also. I'll see you later, in time for dinner."

"That will be fine, if I'm not too much of a bother. Having you take care of me seems to be getting to be a habit."

"Don't always be thinking that you are a bother. I'm glad to take care of you, little one, until you can take care of yourself."

She stood watching him through a crack in her door until he turned into his own room, then she shut the door and turned away with a sigh.

"I'm afraid I'll never want you to stop taking care of me," she said to herself. "Oh, Jimmie, I wonder if you know how much I care for you!"

In so short a time love had come to her. Their chance acquaintance had become infinitely more than friendship to her. It had come so suddenly and in such a short time that it left her bewildered. She knew nothing about this man. She didn't know whether he was married or single. She only knew that she loved him. It startled her when she became aware of it and it brought a sense of fear. She knew that he had no interest in her other than pity and she realized that after his business in the city was finished, she would perhaps never see him again. When she was able to look after herself, there would be no reason for him to take up any more of his time with her.

She slipped off her dress and lay down, but she could not sleep. Why did she have to be such a little idiot, to fall in love with the first stranger she had met when there had been other boys she had known all her life who had loved her and had wanted to marry her? One of them, especially, after her mother had died and he knew that she was going to live in New Orleans, had begged her to marry him and let him take care of her, even though she had told him that she did not love him. She couldn't do that, though it would have solved all her problems. When she married, she wanted to marry for love, not just for a home and security. Now she had given her love to a man who would possibly never know that he had her love, who perhaps was already in love with someone or even married to someone else, a man who would soon be gone from her life, taking her heart and her hope of happiness with him.

CHAPTER 5

JAMES WAS PROVOKED with himself that his interest in Faith was increasing. Though he was impatient to get her affairs settled and to be free of his self-imposed obligation to look after her, he knew that his interest in her as an attractive girl was growing. He did not want this to happen. There was no place in his life for interest in anyone, much less a girl. He had a task to perform and until that was accomplished, he could not let anything interfere.

He would have to be closely associated with this helpless girl until her affairs were settled, but he determined that he would keep his interest entirely on impersonal grounds. He admitted that it would be hard not to be touched by those appealing gray eyes and her childish trust in him. Little did he know that that trust had grown into love. He would have been aghast at the knowledge.

He had not thought of his own attractiveness. He had never considered that, for he was not vain and he did not realize how attractive he was to the feminine eye. He was extremely good looking, with brown hair which insisted upon waving most provokingly across his forehead. His dark brown eyes under the straight brows, and the square chin gave him a look of determination and of strength. No one could guess that this strength and determination had been channeled to such a terrible goal.

He had had only one hint of romance in his life. This was in his last year of high school. One of the elected beauties of the class had made a determined effort to capture him. He had been attracted to her, for she was lovely, but when she made it so plain that she wanted his love, he lost interest in her. Even then he had set himself for the grim task ahead. After that he would not date another girl for fear that love might creep into his life and hinder his plan for revenge. He did not realize that this plan had embittered his whole life and had almost destroyed what promised to be a character which would enable him to accomplish something worthwhile in life.

When he left Faith at her door he put all thoughts of her out of his mind. He went downstairs to the telephone directory and began to search it for any Martins who might be there. He ran over the list carefully, copying down the names. He found many Martins and a number of Thomas Martins. He jotted down these first, with their addresses. Then he wrote down the others. The name was common, but he wanted every name. He knew that the man he sought might have changed a part of his name, if not all of it. That was the thing he feared, that he had changed his name so completely that he would never be able to find him.

He decided that he would call at the residence or office of each man on his list to be sure whether or not he resembled the man he sought. He took out the newspaper clipping with the man's picture in it that his mother had kept from the time of the trial. It was a clear likeness of the man he sought. He was thankful for that. Thomas Martin was a heavy set man with a rather large mouth, a prominent nose and deep set eyes. James studied the face carefully. He realized that the man was much older now and that perhaps he had changed much, but he felt that he would recognize him even if he had changed. He would know him instinctively when they met.

There was still an hour or so before time to meet Faith

for dinner, so he decided to go to the home of the Martin who lived nearest. He had a map of the city and he saw that this address was within walking distance. He expected that the man would be at home, for it was after five. As he drew near the house he became tense and nervous. What if this were the man and his search would be ended this soon? His tension was tinged with dread.

The house was a pretentious one in the Garden District, one of the well-kept ones, smaller than those which had been diverted to rooming houses or other purposes. His nervousness increased as he mounted the steps and rang the bell. A maid opened the door and looked at him inquiringly.

"I came to see Mr. Martin on business. I wonder if he is at home?" he asked her.

"I'm sorry, sir," the maid replied, "but Mr. Martin is dying and he can't see anyone."

"But my business is important, not only to him, but to his family," James insisted. "It concerns his estate."

He couldn't let this man slip out into eternity without getting the chance to look at him. If he didn't succeed, he might never know whether his intended victim had escaped him through death. Death in bed was too easy a way out, he thought grimly.

"Would you tell me what age Mr. Martin is?" he asked on a sudden inspiration. "Perhaps I have the wrong man. All I had was his name and I chose this address at random from the telephone book."

"He's old, almost ninety," the maid told him.

"I don't want to be a nuisance," he said in his most ingratiating manner, "but perhaps there is a picture of him somewhere that I could see. I assure you it's important."

"There's an oil painting of him in the library," she said, "but it's an old one painted when he was a young man."

"Could I see it? If he's not the man I'm looking for, then I'll leave without disturbing the family. Otherwise I must insist upon seeing him or his nearest relative."

Reluctantly the maid led him into the room and showed him the painting. He saw at once that this was not the man he sought. This man was thin and blond and he wore a mustache. His face was kind and the eyes, light blue, looked out at one with frankness and good humor. He was glad that this was not the man and he turned to the maid with a smile.

"I'm sorry to have bothered you," he said, "but this is not the Mr. Martin I seek. I shall have to try elsewhere."

She let him out and he walked back to the rooming house. He could strike that name off his list.

Faith was waiting for him in the living room and they went out together. She was rested and radiant and he forgot for the present his sinister quest. He was glad he had her with him when he ate. It was much better than eating alone. She was in a gay mood and babbled cheerfully, more talkative than she had ever been. He did not know that she was exerting herself to talk of inconsequential things, so that he would not suspect that her heart did a little flip flop every time his eyes met hers, that, now that she had admitted to herself that she loved him, she could not keep her eyes off of him. She felt that there was little time left, perhaps, when she could be with him, and she wanted to extract every little happiness when they were together.

She asked him innumerable questions about the city and then about himself when he was small.

"I'm just curious," she explained, "to know what kind of little boy you were. You seem serious now, as if you had the weight of the world on your shoulders. I wonder if you were always such a serious person. Were you?"

He was startled at her question. He did have the weight of the world on his shoulders. At least it seemed so and that weight had seemed to grow more heavy since he had met her. He was beginning to be sorry that he had harbored this determination for revenge, but it was too late now to be sorry. He had dedicated his life to it and he would not turn back.

He saw that she was waiting for his answer and he spoke slowly and carefully, trying to appear more cheerful than he felt.

"No, I wasn't always such a serious person. I was happy while my father lived. I adored him and we had some wonderful times together. He planned wonderful things for us to do when I grew a little older. He was going to take me to the far places of the world and I would see strange sights that I never imagined existed.''

His eyes grew misty and his thoughts wandered once more to the past while he lived again in memory those scenes of his childhood before tragedy threw out its grim hand and brought disaster.

"And you never did get to those far places, did you?'' she asked sympathetically as she saw the look of sadness upon his face.

"No. My father died after months of suffering and my mother had to work hard until I was old enough to take over and help her. Then she died and I was left alone, as you were. Wasn't that enough to make me serious? Things like that rob one of a cheerful nature, for the joy of living has been taken away.''

"I understand," she said softly. "I've had enough to make me sad and to take away the desire to live, but you have helped to dispel the sadness and make me want to live. You've proved to be a helpful person. Friend, I should say, for you have been a real friend in need.''

"Rather a boorish one, I'm afraid, but I do want to be a real friend in need. Of course you should want to live. There's much in life for you, for you're so young and pretty that I'm sure before long you'll find someone who can make you happier than you ever thought you could be.''

"That would be wonderful.''

She would not meet his eyes. He must not know that she had already met the one who could make her happier than she had ever thought she could be. But how could she ever hope to be happy after he had gone out of her life without even knowing that he was taking her heart with him? How long did it take a person to get over a heartache such as this would be? Would it last forever or would there be someone else who would take his place? No one could ever do that! She turned to him and smiled bravely.

"That same thing could happen to you. I hope it does,

for I do want you to be happy again. But perhaps you've already met that someone. Perhaps you're already married."

She tried to keep her voice as indifferent as she could manage. He could not possibly know how she hung upon his answer.

He laughed mirthlessly. "No, I'm not married. I've never had time for romance. There was too much to occupy my time and thoughts. My mother was ill for a long time before she died and I took care of her until she had to be taken to the hospital. She had tuberculosis."

He did not add that she also had a broken heart.

"I'm sorry," she murmured, but in her heart she was glad that there was no one else. But even if there was no one, how could she ever hope to be the one to bring him happiness? He did not even think of her as a person he could love. She was just someone he was kind enough to help. When that was finished, he would no longer even be interested in her. She sighed in spite of herself and they finished the meal in silence.

CHAPTER 6

IT SEEMED AGES TO JAMES before Faith was finally put in possession of what little her aunt had left. There was nothing but the furniture and a small savings account. When she was finally put in charge and the key to the house was handed to her, she asked James if he would go with her while she looked over her aunt's belongings and decided what to do with them. He agreed, trying not to show how reluctant he was to give up more of his time, and they went to the house together.

He had decided that while he was being delayed so long he had better try to get a position somewhere, since he did not know how long he would be in the city. He put in his application with several concerns and waited anxiously to hear from them.

Though Faith had never been in the house before, still the place seemed to speak of her aunt's presence. When she opened some of the drawers and saw the little personal belongings, tears came to her eyes and she struggled to keep from crying. She came across a few pictures of her when she was a child. She handed them to James.

"That's the kind of scrawny little kid I was," she remarked.

He glanced at the photographs and then at her and a tender smile flitted across his lips.

"You might have been scrawny but you looked like a little angel. Were you as angelic as you look in these pictures?"

"I'm afraid I wasn't," she admitted. "But Mother thought I was. When I grew older and became so indifferent to the Lord, I'm sure she must have changed her mind."

"Unless you plan to live here, I think you'd better sell everything you don't want to keep. You wouldn't have any room for any of this furniture in a rooming house and storage is expensive," he said as they went through the house.

"I couldn't live here," she said. "Everywhere I went I would see my aunt and I couldn't bear it. When Mother died I wanted to get out of that house as quickly as I could. Everywhere I turned I would see things that reminded me of her and brought back all the pain of missing her."

"I understand," he agreed as his eyes became serious.

How he wished his mother were living now! If she were, he would not be on this wild scheme of revenge and there would be more peace in his heart than he could ever hope to have again.

Faith decided to give her aunt's clothes to a poor family in the neighborhood that the lady next door had told her about. The furniture was finally sold through a secondhand furniture dealer. James felt that she was getting only a pittance of the real value of it, but they both decided that this was the easiest and quickest way to dispose of it.

When at last the house was empty and was cleaned, and the remainder of the rent paid, she turned the keys over to the landlord and that chapter of her life was ended.

"Now I'll look for a position somewhere," she said as they went back to the rooming house. "I'll try to keep the money I have for a rainy day, and I'll feel much better now that I do have a little more. I won't be jittery whenever I spend a dime."

"I'm beginning to feel that way," he said. "I shall get

42

something to do as soon as possible, now that your affairs are attended to.''

"I thought you came here on a business trip,'' she said, surprised.

"I did, but I didn't say that it would bring me any money immediately. I've been delayed, so while I'm waiting I'll try to get something to do.''

"I've been the cause of that delay,'' she said with a worried frown. "I'm sure I have and I'm sorry.''

"Don't let that worry you. You haven't delayed me enough to amount to anything. I'm not at all sorry.''

"I'm glad you're going to stay here for a while. I was afraid you'd be leaving soon and I was beginning to feel lonesome already. You're the only friend I have, remember.''

"I'll be sticking around for a while,'' he told her with a smile, "so don't feel lonesome yet. By the time I'm ready to leave, you'll have lots of friends. You'll be able to meet them when you go to work.''

"I don't want any other friends as long as I have you.''

The words slipped out, for she was thinking aloud. As soon as she had said them and saw the startled look on his face, she realized the blunder she had made.

"I shouldn't have said that,'' she stammered, while the color flooded her face. "What I mean is that I've been so well satisfied with your friendship since you've been such a comfort and such a help that I haven't felt the need of making other friends. It is hard for me to make new friends. I know that I shall, though, when I get out where I can meet people, but I shall always keep you at the top of the list.''

She gave him a smile and he nodded without replying. She knew that she had only made matters worse, for she saw the disturbed look in his eyes. She wondered if he had guessed the truth and fear filled her at the thought that he might have. If he had, then he might avoid her or perhaps not be so friendly, for fear that she might be pursuing him.

"I think I shall go down in the French Quarter and see if I can get a job in one of those antique shops. I'd love to work there with all those lovely things. I saw a sign in one of the windows saying that they wanted a salesgirl. What do you think about it?''

She was anxious for him to forget her blunder.

"If that is what you want and if it pays enough," he replied. "It might do for a start until you can find something better. They may want references. I never thought about that before," he added dubiously.

"I never thought about that either," she said. "Even if I had references, they might not do me any good in this place, since my home is so far away."

He had been thinking about the same thing for his own needs. He had references, but he did not know whether they would be any good here.

They went to the shop where she had seen the sign and she was overjoyed when she found that the place had not been filled and that she could have the job. She told the owner of the place the truth about herself and he accepted her without demanding any references. The salary would not be large, but it would be sufficient until she could find something better.

"That's a big load off my mind," she sighed as they left the shop. She was to start work at the beginning of the following week.

When they returned to the rooming house, James found a letter from one of the firms he had contacted, requesting an interview. He left at once to seek that interview. The position was with a large shipping concern. He obtained the position and was to start work the next day. The man whose position he was to fill had died just a few days before.

When he returned to his room he got out his list of Martins and looked it over. There would be less time to interview the men on the list now that he was working. Faith had really been a hindrance to his plans but he did not regret it. He had enjoyed being with her more than he had thought possible and more than he realized until now, when the time had come when they would not see so much of each other. It had been a long time since he had had any companionship

44

with a girl and he found it a new and fascinating experience. She seemed such a child in her helplessness and her dependence upon him that he could scarcely realize she was as old as she was. He conceded to himself that he had enjoyed having her depend upon him even though in the beginning he had resented being bothered with her.

He had thought that before now he would either have found Thomas Martin or he would have been forced to concede that the man was no longer in the city, or, if he was, that he had changed his name, making it impossible for James to find him. He felt now that there was no hurry. Since he had a job he could take his time to continue the search.

He would have time now to plan what he would do if he found his victim. Until now he had not even tried to think of a plan. While his mother was living there was no need to plan, for it had been a nebulous but grim fact in his thinking. Now that he had time to think, he might work out a plan.

If he found this man, just how could he make him suffer before he put an end to his evil life? He would not shoot him, for then death would be too quick and too easy. And a shot could be heard. He must think of a way to get this man alone and in his power. Then he would tell him why he was going to kill him. While his victim was waiting in terror for death, he would relate in detail all the years of suffering his father and mother had endured.

It was a horribly fantastic scheme that he was brooding over, reminiscent of the old days of feuds in the mountains of the east or of torture by the Indians in the early days of the west. How he would kill his victim he did not know, but he was determined to work out some plan that would be sure to succeed.

Suddenly the horror of this thing swept over him and he shuddered in spite of himself. He did not realize how this violent hatred had tinged his whole life, nor did he realize that if he let it grow within him to fruition, it would embitter his whole nature and wreck his life. He had dedicated himself to this and he would not give up until he had either accomplished his purpose or was convinced that he could never find his man.

He looked over the list and decided to try to find the second man on that list. This man had an office near his place of employment and he decided that he would try to find him during his lunch hour at the first opportunity.

A knock on the door interrupted his thoughts and he put the list away and answered the knock. It was Faith.

"I didn't know whether you were in or not," she said. "I'll wait for you downstairs if you're not ready to eat now. That is, if you still want me to go with you."

"I'll be right down. And why shouldn't I want you to go with me?" he asked with a smile. "Has the world suddenly changed since you've gotten a job?"

"I just thought that now you wouldn't need to bother with me any longer and you might want to be by yourself for a change."

"I'd still rather have company when I eat," he assured her. "I'll be right down as soon as I wash."

He joined her and they went to their usual place. While they waited for their order he told her that he was going to work the next day.

"Oh, dear!" she exclaimed. "I'll be all by myself for almost a week. I'll feel as if I've been deserted. I've grown used to having you around to talk to whenever I begin to feel lonesome."

"You'll have time to look in some of the stores," he suggested. "I've noticed some interesting looking ones down on Canal Street."

"I could do that, but it isn't much fun window shopping alone. But there I go, spreading gloom when I should be glad that you have a job, too. I am, really. But it will seem strange, eating all alone. I'll be talking to myself and pretending that I am talking to you."

"There'll be no need to pretend. I'll still have to eat. We can still have breakfast and dinner together and we may even manage to have lunch together often. You won't get rid of me that easily."

"I was afraid you'd be wanting to get rid of me."

She let her eyes drop, for she could not meet his suddenly intent gaze. Once more she had blundered. Perhaps he had guessed how much she loved him. But he could never guess how much she cared! How could he ever possibly guess that?

"You'll be finding a pal before long and you'll be giving me the high sign to stay away," he said, breaking the sudden silence.

She smiled. "I'll do my best to look for that person and let you off the hook."

He wondered, as they began their meal, how he would feel if she should do that. There would be a vacancy in his life if she did. He realized now how completely she had filled his life in the short time they had known each other. It would seem strange if he should see her with some other fellow. It wouldn't seem right. It was his right to look after her and to keep those lovely gray eyes free of tears. Where would it all end, he wondered. There was hope for a bright future for her, but for himself — what?

CHAPTER 7

JAMES WAS PLEASED with his job and with his salary. It was more than he had hoped for. He knew that he would need money if he should have to make a quick getaway. He spent many worried hours trying to plan some scheme that would enable him to carry out his plan and make it possible to get away before the murder was discovered.

The full horror of the thing bore down upon him more strongly, the terrible reality that he was planning a cold-blooded, brutal murder, but he fought against it and continued planning, nevertheless. He must do this thing, he must avenge his father's death. If he did not, he would be failing his father and his mother. The man who had done this to them and had escaped punishment by the law must be punished by him. He should not be allowed to live.

He knew nothing of what God had said in His Word that "vengeance is mine, I will repay." He would not have given up if he had known. Since the law had failed to punish the real criminal, he would do what the law had not done.

During the first weeks on his job he was too intent upon getting adjusted to his work to take time to pursue his search, but during his leisure hours when he was alone he thought of nothing else. The more he saw of Faith, however, the more distasteful his scheme became. He tried not to think of her, but his thoughts would wander to her in spite of his every effort. Thoughts of her would intrude upon him while he was studying the map and comparing it with his telephone list. He would throw the map aside in disgust and pick up a book. He had stacked on the table a collection of books from the library. They were all murder or mystery stories. He was interested in following the schemes of murderers and their attempts to outwit the law. His whole mind was becoming more warped as time passed.

Faith was so lonesome during the days that intervened until she was due to go to work, that she was utterly miserable. She had to eat alone at lunch time. Immediately after their brief morning meal, James boarded the bus and she was left alone. She wandered through the stores and saw many things that she would have liked to buy, but she could not afford to spend her money except for necessities. She counted the hours until James would return, and their evening meal was the one bright spot in the long day.

"I'd die of loneliness if I weren't going to work soon," she remarked. "I've gotten so used to having you with me that I feel lost all by myself."

"You'll be much happier when you find some girl that you can pal around with," he told her.

"How do you know what it takes to make a girl happy?" she asked. "I don't suppose you've ever felt as lonely as I do. Men are different."

He looked at her while a quizzical smile spread over his lips. "We're human and I suppose we get just as lonely as you do. I've been lonely." His face became serious. "I may know more in the future about loneliness than you could ever know."

He was sorry he had let those words slip. Their friendship had come to mean so much to him that he looked forward each day to the time when they could be together. He was thinking of the time which might be soon, when he would have to leave her and never see her again. The thought brought bitterness to his very soul.

"There's something worrying you," she said gravely as she looked at him with concern. "Would you mind telling me what it is? You have helped me so many times that I wish I could help you."

"It's nothing," he said, brushing his hand across his eyes as if he were brushing away an unpleasant scene. "I was just wondering where I would go and what I would do when my business here is finished."

"Won't you be going back to your home out west?"

"No. I have no home there any more. When I'm finished here, I'll be going somewhere, but there is no place where I really want to go."

"Then why not stay here?" she suggested hopefully.

"I don't believe I would like that."

His eyes became clouded again and a sigh escaped him which she heard but of which he was not aware. It would indeed be lonely for him when he became a wanderer. Perhaps he would never be able to find anyone with whom he could be friends. He would be afraid to make friends. He could never be too intimate with anyone for fear that they might connect him with his crime. He knew that the law's long arm was far reaching and that it never gave up searching for its victim. He would be a hunted man for the rest of his life.

This was his weakest moment, when he was almost ready to give up this mad scheme of vengeance and live a normal life, the life he had been born to live. But the memory of his mother's face and her agonized voice when she told him that his father had died, the months of suffering while her life was slowly ebbing away, made him forget this moment of weakness while he grimly determined to carry on.

She saw the shadow deepen on his face and longed to say something that would remove it. She looked at him silently while he seemed unaware of her presence, loving him and grieving that before long they would be parted, perhaps forever.

A few weeks later he decided to look up another Martin on his list. He took the bus to the address and discovered that it was a small double cottage, common in that part of the city. He stood outside for a while, looking at the house and wondering just what he should do and say when he rang the bell. He did not think that this could be the home of the man he sought. He would not be living in a house as small as this one. He had made too much money in settling the business after James' father had been sent to prison. He must see the man, however, just to be sure. He rang the bell and waited impatiently for someone to answer. A young man not much older than himself opened the door. He eyed James silently, then asked him what he wanted.

"I'm looking for a Mr. Thomas Martin," James told him. "My firm sent me to interview him about some insurance he took out a number of years ago." It was a plausible lie and could not cause any suspician.

"You must mean my uncle," the young man told him. "He used to live here and the phone is listed in his name. I'm John Irving. Mr. Martin was my mother's brother."

"Would you mind telling me where he is now?" James asked.

"He lives in Mobile. Would you like to have his address?"

"If you don't mind," James replied.

"Come in and I'll get it for you," Irving offered.

James followed him inside and waited in the living room while the young man went to get the address. He looked about him at the simply furnished room and he saw a picture hanging on the wall opposite him. It was an enlarged photograph of a man, perhaps sixty, rather stout, with wide mouth and deep set eyes. He caught his breath as he stared at the picture. This could be the man he sought! He was both elated and stunned now that he thought he had found his man. Just then the young man returned.

"Is this your uncle's picture?" James asked.

"Yes. How did you know?"

"We had a picture of him in our files in the office, taken some time ago," James replied. "I'm fortunate if I have found him so soon. He has been out of touch with our office for so long that we did not have his present address.''

The thought came to him that this man might remember him when he learned that his uncle had been murdered. A shudder of fear and revulsion swept through him, but he managed to smile at Irving as he took the address, thanked him and left.

He would not be able to go to Mobile until the next weekend. He could make the trip in a day. If this were the man he sought, he would be moving to Mobile. And he would not see Faith any more. He would miss her and now that the parting seemed imminent he realized how much he would miss her. He had not counted on this and he was sorry that he had ever met her. But she had given him many pleasant hours that he had not thought possible. He would regret that parting and the thought of what the trip might mean to his future made him reluctant to take it. But he must. He could not rest until he knew.

He did not tell Faith of his intended trip until the night before he was to leave. He had Saturday off and planned to go then. If he had to stay overnight, he would still be able to get back to work on Monday.

They had had dinner and were on their way home. They stopped for a moment and sat in a corner of the steps.

''It's too early to go to bed,'' he said and drew her down beside him. ''Let's sit here for a little while.'' He turned to her and gave her a smile. Then the smile faded and he became serious. He hated to tell her just now, but he had to. ''I'm going to walk out on you tomorrow, little one.''

''Walk out on me!'' she echoed aghast. ''You mean you're going away?''

He nodded.

''You're going away! Oh, Jimmie!'' A sob choked her.

She had never called him Jimmie before. In fact, he could not remember her ever having called his name before. The look of utter woe upon her face touched him and wakened something within him that was new and entirely unsuspected.

''Don't let it upset you,'' he said soothingly. ''Perhaps

it will be only for a day. I'll be back before you have time to miss me."

She uttered a deep sigh and gave him a reproachful look.

"That was mean of you to frighten me so. Please don't do it again."

He leaned nearer and looked into her eyes that were filled with tears.

"Would you really miss me that much if I should go away?"

"Of course," she responded, trying to regain her composure. "I have no other friends and I really would be lonesome, especially at meal time." She tried to smile, but the smile refused to come.

He leaned back against the step and caught his knee in his hands.

"I would be lonesome without you," he told her. "But I may have to go away sooner than I expected. It depends upon how things turn out on this trip. I shall hate to leave you, little one," he added with a tender note in his voice. "It's been fun, taking care of you. I'll be better satisfied, though, knowing that you have a job and a good place to stay."

"Please let me know ahead of time if you have to go. Don't spring it on me as you did tonight. Give me a little time to get used to being without you."

"I will," he assured her.

"Will you write to me when you go away?" she asked.

He was startled at her question and the realization of what would follow when he did go away. He could not even write to her. He would never know what became of her after he left her, whether she would find someone else to take his place or what would happen to her. The thought that she would find someone else gave him a pang of jealousy. It swept over him with a sickening sense of frustration and loss. He loved her. Why hadn't he seen this coming long before now? He had been too engrossed in his obsession to even realize that love had come into his life while hate was poisoning that life and leading him to destruction.

He turned to her and tried to smile but it was a dismal failure.

"I'm a poor hand at writing, but I'll do my best," he told her, but he knew that he was lying. When he left her she would never hear from him again. She would suffer, just as he would suffer, for he knew that she cared for him. He realized it tonight.

"Let's go," he said heavily. "I'm tired and this step is getting hard."

They rose and as she gazed at him she thought that he could not see the look of adoration that was in her eyes, but he did see. He caught her in his arms and kissed her tenderly. Then he let her go suddenly as if he regretted what he had done.

She stared at him in unbelievable, rapturous joy while she held her clasped hands against her breast.

"Jimmie!" she breathed. "You kissed me!"

He tried to laugh but the laugh would not come.

"Yes, I kissed you. Was that so terrible?"

"No! No! It was wonderful — so — so — wonderful! Oh, Jimmie, did it — did it mean that you care?"

He meant to laugh it off and tell another lie, that the kiss meant nothing, that it was just a good-by, but he could not. When he looked into her rapturous face and saw the joy in her wide eyes, as her lovely face was held up to him, he could not tell her anything but the truth.

He took her in his arms again and whispered, "Yes, it means that I do care, little one. I care a great deal, more than I should care for anyone. I love you, Faith, darling. I love you."

He bent and his lips met hers again. She clung to him with her arms about his neck.

"Oh, Jimmie! How glad I am that you do care! I've loved you for such a long time, it seems, but I never hoped that you would ever care for me. Jimmie! I love you so! I love you so!"

He took her arms from about his neck and released her almost roughly.

"I have no right to love you," he said harshly. "Just forget what I said."

"What do you mean?" she cried in distress at the sudden change in him. "Why have you no right to love me? You said there was no one else."

"I have no room in my life for love," he told her.

In that moment he drank the very dregs of bitterness and despair. He turned away from her while his shoulders drooped in absolute dejection.

She came closer and put her arms around his neck again.

"Please don't turn away from me," she begged. "Let me love you even if there is no room in your life for love. Loving you is all I have and having your love is all I want."

"I must," he said and the words were a moan. "I can't tell you why, so don't ask me, but I must. I love you and perhaps I always shall, but there never can be anything between us, so just try to forget that I kissed you and forget what I said."

He tore away from her clinging arms and ran up the steps and into the house.

She followed him slowly while the tears coursed down her cheeks. She had mounted to the dizzy heights of joy and had been plunged into the depths of despair in so short a time that she could not bear it. She went to her room and dropped onto the bed where she lay sobbing. No matter what the reasons for his words might be, they were final. She could not doubt that. He would soon be gone and she would be left alone to think of what might have been and to wonder what sinister shadow lay between them. All her life, perhaps, she would wonder and would never know. It seemed more than she could bear, yet she knew that she must go on living no matter how great was the burden of sorrow.

She got up and turned on the light and got ready for bed. The night seemed dark indeed, the darkest she had ever known.

CHAPTER 8

JAMES LEFT EARLY the next morning before Faith was up. He slipped a note under her door telling her that he was sorry he could not have breakfast with her, but that he would have to catch an early train. This was not true, but he did not want to see her again after last night. He must have time to gain strength to control his emotions until he could master the desire to hold her in his arms again and feel the touch of her lips upon his.

Perhaps it would be better to move to another rooming house as he had planned in the beginning if the man he met in Mobile was not the one he was looking for. It would be hard to be near her and to continue their relationship as mere friends. It would be almost impossible, for, even if he could conquer his own desire he knew that the sight of her pleading eyes and the knowledge that he was making her suffer would be almost more than he could bear.

He was hoping that this Martin might be the man he sought so that he could get the matter over and get away where he would never see her again. Seeing her every day and knowing that they could never belong to each other would be torture.

As the train sped along the coast where he could see the

wave-lashed waters, he felt that he was being driven by some demon force within him which was impelling him to his doom. The meeting ahead and the task to which he had dedicated his life became more abhorrent each mile he traveled. He wanted to get it over and go on to whatever fate might await him when the deed was done. He could not keep from thinking of the love he had turned his back upon and the happiness which that love would bring and which he was deliberately throwing away for a future which he dreaded to contemplate.

He tried to sleep so he would not think, but every time he closed his eyes Faith's face appeared before him. The tear-drenched eyes with their pleading look and the echo of her voice would ring within his memory as she begged him to just let her love him even if he had no place in his life for love.

He opened his eyes to shut out the sight of that face which had become so dear to him, dearer now that the parting would perhaps be so near. He scanned the landscape with listless eyes that scarcely saw, the tall marsh grasses that covered the land between the train and the waters that led to the Gulf, the swarms of black marsh birds that flew up from the ground and lined the telephone wires, then flew away again, black dots against the blue sky.

When the train stopped at stations along the coast, children gathered around with small crates of crabs or shrimp imbedded in moss, offering them for sale. One small boy held up a string of fish, hopefully waiting for someone to buy them. James could not resist a smile at the little fellow's efforts to dispose of his catch, and he wondered what the coach would smell like during the next hour or so if those fish came aboard without ice or other means of preservation.

As soon as he reached Mobile, he took a cab to the address of Thomas Martin, His heart beat with excitement and dread bore down upon him as he reached the house and got out, telling the driver to wait for him.

With perspiration dripping down his face, he walked up the steps and rang the bell. The house was much more pretentious than the one this man had occupied in New Orleans and he wondered what sudden burst of prosperity had made the change possible. He did not have long to speculate, for a maid answered his ring.

"Is Mr. Martin in?" he asked.

"Yes, he is," she replied. "Who wishes to see him?"

"He doesn't know me. My name is John Travers. I've come to see him on business."

She invited him in and went to get Mr. Martin. James waited nervously and presently Mr. Martin came in and looked inquiringly at him. James rose and approached to get a better look at him. He saw at once that this man did not resemble the newspaper cut. He wondered why that picture he had seen in New Orleans looked so much like it when the original of the picture did not.

"Mr. Martin, I'm John Travers," he said. "I'm looking for a Mr. Martin who lived in New Orleans and when I went to your former address your nephew sent me here."

"What is it you want?" Mr. Martin asked. "Please sit down."

"I represent the U & V Insurance Company," James told him. "We have a paid-up policy for Mr. Thomas Martin which the company has had for some time. The owner of that policy did not leave his latest address with us and the company has not been able to reach him. We would like to get the matter finished so that our books may be cleared of the transaction. They sent me to New Orleans to see if I could locate him."

"I'm not the man you want," Mr. Martin replied. "I never have had any insurance with that company. I'm sorry you have had the trip for nothing."

He rose to indicate that the interview was at an end and James was forced to rise also. He could not leave without putting one more question to the man.

"I saw your photograph in your nephew's house," he said. "It doesn't look very much like you. I wonder why. Would you mind telling me? That photograph looked like the man I was seeking."

"That was not my picture," Martin told him. "That was my brother's picture. He died several years ago. He was Ted Martin."

"Did he ever live in Arizona?" James asked. He was determined to be sure that the dead man was not the one he sought. "It was there that the policy was taken out."

"No, none of us has ever lived anywhere outside of New Orleans. I came here to Mobile after my brother died to look after some business and we both liked it here and decided to move here. We lived in that little old house in New Orleans because my wife had lived there all her life and hated to leave it. I was glad to get rid of it. My wife is an invalid and this house is more comfortable."

"I'm sorry if I have bothered you," James remarked as they went to the door.

"It was no bother," Mr. Martin replied politely.

James felt disappointed and yet relieved as he left the house. When he realized that the man's wife was an invalid, he thought how terrible it would be if this were the man he had to kill. Cold sweat broke out upon him and a chill swept through him even though the day was warm. He hoped that if he did find Martin, there would be no invalid wife to arouse his sympathy.

The enormity of the crime he was planning bore down upon him as he neared the depot and waited for the return train. He felt more surely than ever that he was being driven on by some force he could not master, to do a deed against which his whole being was beginning to revolt. It had not seemed so terrible when it was only a vague dream, but now that it was becoming a horrible reality, he wondered how he could have lived with this thing all these years. But there was no turning back. He must go on to the task he had set himself. He wondered what the end would be. He was beginning to hope that he would never find his man, but he crushed that dim hope. He could not be disloyal to the memory of his father. He didn't stop to think that his father would never have wanted revenge at so high a price. If he could have spoken from the grave, he would have told him to forget hate and to live so that he would have the best in life, the life that they had planned together.

When he reached the rooming house he hurried in, hoping to get to his room without letting Faith know he had returned. He didn't want to meet her yet. He wanted time to get control of himself and plan what he would do.

He met her in the hall as she was leaving her room. When she saw him she uttered a glad little cry.

"Jimmie! You've come back! How glad I am! I was just going out to get something to eat, but now I won't have to go alone."

"I'm not hungry but I am tired," he said. "You'd better go on without me."

His heart smote him at her look of disappointment. The glad light left her eyes and her mouth drooped at the corners. She looked like a child getting ready to cry.

"All right, if you don't want to go with me," she said in a hurt little voice, then she turned and walked slowly down the hall.

He couldn't stand to hurt her, nor could he conquer the desire to be with her, so he called to her.

"Wait. I'll go with you. I'll eat, just to please you, even though I'm not hungry."

"I'm so glad," she whispered as he caught up with her. "Now I'll be happy again." She gave him a bright smile.

She caught hold of his arm as they walked up the street and he held it close to his side.

"We should know this menu from memory after all this time," she remarked as he gave their order. "Was your business a success?"

"No, it wasn't." His face was so serious that she attributed it to disappointment.

"I'm sorry if you were disappointed, but I'm glad that it wasn't a success, because that means you'll be here a while longer, doesn't it?"

He nodded. If she only knew why he would be here longer, her love would turn to loathing. He gazed at her hungrily and she returned his look with a look of adoration that swept away his gloom.

"You're adorable," he whispered.

"I love you, Jimmie," she murmured while her eyes were alight with the joy that enveloped her at his words.

"It's heavenly, having you back," she remarked as they were on their way home. "This has been such a long day. It was because I knew you were not here and I was afraid that you would be leaving soon. I still hope that you will like it here well enough never to want to leave."

"Don't hope for that," he advised.

His soul writhed within him. She was dear and her nearness thrilled him with a joy he had never had before and never hoped to have.

"I won't give up hope," she stated stubbornly. "I need something to cheer me up and give me hope, for this job isn't what I hoped it would be."

"What's wrong with it?" he asked with concern.

"I thought it would be wonderful to work among those lovely antiques and that beautiful jewelry, but that manager is a crabbed old antique himself and his bookkeeper is even worse. They both seem to have it in for me. Nothing I do is ever right. All he ever lets me do is wait on customers who want to look at jewelry. I didn't want to tell you, but it's getting me down."

"We'll look for another job," he said encouragingly. "That's not the only place in town that can use a lovely little salesgirl like you."

She laughed happily. "I knew you'd say something that would help. Now everything will be all right."

When they reached her room, they paused a moment at her door.

"Goodnight, Jimmie, dear," she whispered. "It's good to know that you are not far away."

He put his arms around her and drew her to him. He kissed her almost roughly, then released her and turned away.

"Jimmie, I love you," she said in low tones as he turned

61

away. "Just let me love you, please!"

"Don't! Don't!" he cried in a voice of agony as he hurried down the hall to his room and shut the door behind him.

CHAPTER 9

THE HOT SUMMER and the pleasant fall passed and winter set in, with cold, rainy days and wind-swept nights. James saw little of Faith except on weekends. He was working at night and quite often on Saturdays during the rush period at the office. He was glad for an excuse to break off their constant association. He left for work before she was up and got a cup of coffee and doughnuts at the French Market on his way to his office. If she felt that he was avoiding her, she did not reproach him or complain when they were together. She just seemed happy to be with him.

During the summer they had been in the habit of going to one of the parks in the afternoon on Sunday or else out to the lake where they sat in the shade and watched the sailboats skimming along the water, but now he left her after dinner. He pleaded work that he had to finish and that he was too tired to go anywhere, so she was left to her loneliness while he tried to read or sleep.

Faith knew that he was avoiding her and she spent many unhappy hours wondering what it was that separated them. She believed that he had told her the truth when he had said that he was not married. But perhaps he was divorced and his wife might have some hold upon him that made him feel he had no right to her love. She could see that he was worried and that he was suffering from some hidden sorrow. She feared that she would never be able to solve the mystery.

She had asked him several times what was worrying him but he refused to talk about it and he became irritated when she tried to cheer him. She could not know, of course, that her efforts were like a knife probing a wound.

One day, after she had spent a miserable night trying to solve the mystery, she asked him again if he were married. It was after he had impulsively laid his hand upon hers as it lay on the table near him and looked at her with such desperate longing that it brought a stab of pain to her heart.

"Jimmie, what is it that keeps you from me? Please tell me," she begged.

"I don't want to talk about it," he told her harshly. "I told you before that I didn't. Why can't you accept things as they are and not worry because they can never be any different?"

"Because I love you so much," she said in a voice that trembled in spite of her efforts to keep it steady. "I want to be happy in your love and I want you to be happy. I know you're not happy. You said you loved me. Were you telling the truth or were you just stringing me along? Tell me, Jimmie."

"It was the truth," he said slowly, as if the words were forced from him against his will.

"Then have you stopped loving me? If you have, please tell me. I'd rather we didn't see each other ever again, if you're just hanging on because you know I want to be with you."

"I haven't changed," he said heavily, "but it would be better if we didn't see each other, for nothing can ever come of love between us."

"Tell me the truth. Is there someone else out of the past who stands between us?"

Her words gave him such a sudden start that he could not conceal his surprise. He recovered himself quickly. How true her words were! Someone from the past did stand between them and that someone would always be there to stand

64

between them. His shoulders sagged and he looked at her with such wretchedness that it brought tears to her eyes. She had seen his start and the fleeting look of fear that shone in his eyes and she felt that she must have hit upon the truth.

"Is it true that you are not married?" she asked as he did not speak.

"It's true. I told you the truth. I'm not married and I never shall be," he added so slow that she could scarcely hear him.

"And you're not divorced?" she probed, trying desperately to get at the truth.

"No, Faith, I'm not divorced. Stop trying to quiz me. I don't want to talk about it, so let's let the matter drop."

"Just tell me one more thing, Jimmie," she said as her wistful gaze met his. "Would you rather stop seeing me altogether? If you would prefer to have it that way, please be honest with me and I'll do whatever you want me to do."

There was such a surrender and yet such heartbreak in her voice as her eyes held his that once more she reminded him of a little lost kitten, fearing to be turned astray again and cringing against that possibility.

He put out his hand again and seized hers and held it so tightly that it hurt her.

"I want to be with you. I want you! I want you! God help me, I want you!" It was a cry of despair. "But I can never have you. You would be better off if you never saw me again. Let's go."

He rose and she followed him. They walked along in silence until they reached the rooming house. She stopped at her door and he was going to pass on to his room, but she laid her hand upon his arm and stopped him.

"Jimmie, just let me say this and I promise never to question you again. If there is something in your past that you have done, no matter what it was, I don't care. Even if you killed someone, it wouldn't make any difference to me. I would love you just the same. If you were running away from the law and had to flee to the ends of the earth, I would be willing to go with you and to share whatever fate you might face. I love you that much, Jimmie."

He looked at her a moment, speechless, then he caught her hand and pressed it to his lips.

"God bless you!" he whispered, then turned and left her standing with white face and eyes that suddenly filled with tears.

She went inside and dropped upon a chair. She felt that she had hit upon the truth. He must have committed some crime. That did not matter now. The past was gone and the future was ahead of them. If he could only know how glad she would be to face that future with him, no matter what it might hold! But she would never be able to do that. She couldn't beg him to marry her and since he had never given her any hope that he would want her as his wife, there was nothing she could do but grieve and suffer and hope. But hope seemed dim just now.

James shuddered and he felt sick and beaten as he went to his room. How surely she had hit upon the thing that stood between them! He had not killed yet, but he was a potential murderer. He was touched by her willingness to share whatever penalty he might be called upon to pay for the crime which she thought he might have committed. How he wished that he could have her with him if he should be forced to flee from the law! But a murder committed in the past and one which he expected to commit in the future were different matters. The past was not a part of her but this would be. He could never have her, no matter how willing she might be to go with him. He could not be burdened with anyone if he were forced to be a wanderer for the rest of his life.

He was glad that he could not see much of her as his work grew heavier. She took a cold and had to remain in bed for a few days. The landlady was kind and took care of her until she was up again. She did not have a doctor, but even after she was able to return to work a little nagging cough hung on.

James saw how pale she looked and it worried him. Her skin seemed almost transparent and though she insisted that she felt well, he was concerned about her. She had not said anything more about the unpleasant situation at the shop and he had not asked her about it. He was engrossed in his own problems and she did not want to annoy him with her troubles. She searched the want ads but she could not find anything that seemed to be what she needed or what she could do.

James was so busy that he had no time to continue his search. The experience he had had in Mobile made him willing to wait until he had more time. He was anxious to get it over, yet he dreaded what would happen if he did find his man.

Christmas week came and the city assumed a festive air. The light standards on Canal Street were decorated with Christmas trees and huge Santas, red and white candy sticks and other toys, and the stores were brilliant with lights and with nativity scenes displayed upon their front walls. People thronged the stores and the streets were crowded with shoppers.

James suggested that they should go downtown on one of his free nights and wander through the stores. He had not seen her all week and he could not control the longing to be with her. This was a peaceful interlude in his life now that his search had ceased until after the New Year's rush was over. They strolled along Canal Street and through the stores and then ate hamburgers and drank coffee before they returned home.

On Christmas day they decided to have dinner at one of the downtown restaurants famous for its French cuisine. It was a lovely place, the atmosphere of which made them somehow seem very close. Faith fondly admired the dainty corsage Jim had given her for the occasion. They had exchanged gifts that morning. This dinner date was something special.

She gave him a radiant smile. "I shall remember this day as long as I live," she said.

"Dear me!" he exclaimed. "You've a long life ahead of you."

"It will always be a beautiful memory," she repeated, and she spoke with meaning in her voice.

"Your future husband might object to such sentiment," he said playfully.

"There will be no future husband," she said as her serious eyes met his amused gaze. "I shall always belong to you, Jimmie, even though you may be so far away."

Their gayety suddenly departed and they finished the meal in almost complete silence.

The shop where Faith worked was crowded with visitors who would be coming in increasing numbers until after the Mardi Gras season and she worked late every day. She came home exhausted and went to bed as soon as she reached her room. She could not get her strength back and she dragged through the days fighting exhaustion.

James had not seen her for over a week for he was also busy working at the office. One morning he received an urgent telephone call. It was from Faith.

"Jimmie, can you please come?" she wailed. "They have arrested me and I'm in jail."

"What have they arrested you for?" he cried in dismay.

"They say I stole a lot of jewelry." She was crying so that she could scarcely talk. "Please come. They want me to hang up."

"I'll be there as soon as I can get there," he told her. "Don't worry. We'll get you out. And don't cry. Everything will be all right."

He got his hat and coat and after a hurried explanation to his superior in the office, he went outside and hailed a cab.

What on earth had happened that she should be accused of stealing, he wondered. He knew that she was not guilty.

A sudden thought arrested him. The law had a most amazing memory for faces. He wondered if those he would be forced to meet in trying to help her would remember him after he had broken the law. But that was a foolish thought born of his own sense of guilt and fear. He was in the depths of gloom as he reached the prison and mounted the broad steps and went inside.

CHAPTER 10

JAMES GOT TO THE PARISH PRISON as soon as he could and finally obtained permission to see Faith by herself. He was taken upstairs and down the gloomy corridor to a room near where the female prisoners were kept. The matron remained nearby while they talked.

When Faith saw him she burst into tears. Her eyes were red with weeping and the matron remarked that she had been crying ever since she had been committed. He took her in his arms and tried to comfort her. When she had become calm enough to talk she told him what had happened.

"They accused me of stealing a lot of valuable jewelry that had come in on consignment," she said. "You know I didn't steal it, don't you, Jimmie? I couldn't do a thing like that."

"Of course you couldn't," he said, stroking her rumpled hair. She seemed smaller and more fragile than ever as he held her. "What grounds did they have for accusing you?"

"They found a diamond ring from the lot in my coat pocket. It was caught in a corner of the pocket. I don't know how it got there. Someone must have put it there to make them think that I stole the other things. That's what I told them, but no one would believe me. My boss, Mr. Rogers, said that things had been missing ever since I started working there, just little things and he suspected me, but he didn't want to accuse me until he had proof. He's angry because he has to made good that loss, if they don't find the jewelry. They searched me as soon as they brought me here." She began to cry again.

"That's routine work," the matron informed James. "I search all the prisoners to be sure that they don't have any concealed weapons or narcotics."

She had seen James' angry look directed toward her and while she was used to angry looks and accusations, somehow this terrified young prisoner who seemed such a helpless child had aroused her sympathy. She had became hardened in her work and usually was not convinced when a prisoner protested her innocence, for they all did that, but this girl was different. She felt that if this girl had committed a crime, it must have been her first offense and she must have been terribly desperate to have been tempted to commit it.

"I'll get a lawyer and we'll get you out of this in no time at all," James assured her. "Just buck up and try to be brave. I'll come back as soon as I can. Promise not to cry any more. If you keep this up, you'll get sick and that would make matters worse."

"I'll try," she said tremulously and smiled faintly.

He bent and kissed her, then let her go back to the cell with the matron. She gave him a despairing look as she went out and the door closed behind her.

When James got back to the office he asked his office manager if he knew a good lawyer, then he went to see Mr. Rogers at the shop. The man seemed to be in a state of nervous fury. He said that this was the worst blow he had had since he had been in business. He said his insurance policy on burglary had run out recently and he had neglected to have it renewed. This loss would represent more than he could pay and would almost bankrupt him.

James asked him why he had not taken more precautions

against theft if the jewelry was so valuable. His only excuse was negligence.

"I should have known better, but nothing like this has ever happened before. I've had sickness at home and other troubles and I've been so worried that I just let things go. I never should have left that girl in charge of that show case, but I didn't think. I'll beat it out of her if she won't confess where she hid that jewelry."

"If you do, you'll get the beating of your life," James told him. "She didn't steal that jewelry. I'm sure of that."

"Well, I'm sure she did," Rogers argued. "I should have known better than to have hired her. She didn't live here. She was just a drifter. She might have been in trouble with the law somewhere before she came here. That little baby face of hers is a good front for a thief. She sure used me for a sucker."

"That's a lie and I ought to choke it down your throat," James cried furiously. "She's not a thief and she wasn't putting on any front."

"Getting riled up won't help her any," Rogers said. "If you're such a good friend of hers, how do I know that you're not mixed up in this yourself? That girl had one of the rings on her when the police came. It was down in a corner where she overlooked it. What do you say to that?"

"I say that it was a plant," James repeated.

He restrained his anger, for the man's hint that he himself might come under suspicion made him realize that he might be in danger of being accused as an accessory to the crime. If this should happen, he would not only be where he could not help Faith, but it would also endanger the success of the crime he planned.

"Why don't you take a look at that shriveled book-keeper over there?" James asked as he saw the man standing nearby. "He could be the guilty one."

Rogers uttered a short laugh. "Accuse old Tom? I'd as soon accuse myself. He's been with me ever since I started in business. He's got a part interest in this business. Why should he steal from himself?"

"I don't know, but I mean to find out," James said as he left. He phoned the lawyer who had been recommended to him and had a conference with him. He told the lawyer, Mr. Sutton, what his suspicions were and Sutton advised him to hire a detective to trail the bookkeeper. The detective might find something that would prove Faith's innocence before the case came to trial.

James phoned the agency that Sutton had recommended and engaged a detective by the name of Grogan. The price seemed enormously high and he realized with a sinking sensation that his small savings would be terribly reduced. He was not caring about that now, however. His main desire was to get Faith acquitted.

When he returned to the rooming house that evening, a worried and indignant landlady met him in the hall. The police had been there and they had searched Faith's room.

"They told me that she was arrested for stealing a lot of jewelry," she told James. "I don't like things like this to happen in my house, Mr. Thornton. It will give me a bad name. I don't like to ask you to move, but I don't want any unpleasant publicity."

"I'll move as soon as I can find a place," James told her, "if that is what you want. But do let her things stay here for a while. I know that she is innocent and when they acquit her, you'll get a lot of publicity, but it will be good, not bad."

"I'll think it over," she said, mollified. "I like the little girl. She was sweet and seemed like a helpless child. Made me think of my little girl, just her age when she died. I'm glad you're so sure she's innocent. I'd hate to think she could do a thing like that."

"I'll stake my life on her innocence," James declared.

"You think a lot of her, don't you? It was good of you to take her under your wing when she was in trouble."

"I love her and I'm going to marry her," he said slowly.

Marry her! What had he said? How could he marry her? But when the words were out he knew that he would do just that. Just now all thoughts of his scheme for vengeance and murder were banished. When Faith was released, he would marry her and take the consequences, the risk of having her turn from him in loathing, if she learned what he planned to do. They would go away together when his mission had been accomplished, and try to be happy somewhere far from here, even though the shadow of the law might hang over them for the rest of his life.

The landlady gave him a smile and her irritation over the visit of the police vanished suddenly and entirely.

"How romantic!" she exclaimed. "I do hope that you get her out real soon. I'll give you my best front room at no extra cost."

"Then you don't want me to move?" James asked with a faint smile.

"No. You just stay on here and don't worry. I know you'll get her out soon."

They went to Faith's room. It was in shambles. The police had literally torn it apart in their search for the stolen jewelry. He and the landlady straightened it out and then James went to his room. He had forgotten that he had not eaten, but he was too upset to even feel hungry. His sudden declaration that he was going to marry Faith had given him a shock. He had long fought against this desire, but at last it had conquered his determination to overcome it. When she got out, if she got out, he conceded gloomily, she would need him more than ever. She would have no job and, even if she were acquitted, she would have a hard time finding work, for the stigma of that arrest would follow her even after she was free. He put his head in his hands and tried to think clearly, but his thoughts were a confused jumble. Finally he got up and went out to get something to eat, then he went to bed and tried to sleep, but for hours sleep would not come.

He tried to see Faith the next day but was unable to receive permission. He was told that he would have to wait until visiting time. He phoned his lawyer and later that afternoon they both went to the prison. Faith was not crying now, but she looked so pale and wan that she was a pitiful figure. She told her story to the lawyer and he agreed with James that that ring must have been a plant. There was no one else who could be the guilty one but the bookkeeper, but they would have to prove his guilt and that would be hard to prove unless the detective could unearth something.

Faith looked more hopeless than ever when they left her. She asked James to have the landlady send some of her clothes.

"Just one or two of the oldest ones," she told him. "I don't trust those awful women in there. And some of them are so dirty that I won't want to wear anything I've worn here, if I ever get out." Her lip trembled and she was on the verge of tears, but she managed to control them.

His heart was heavy when he left her.

The trial was set for several weeks ahead. Though it seemed an eternity to Faith, in the eyes of the law she was only a name on the court records and no one else was concerned about the delay but James. Mr. Sutton said it was good that the trial was set so far ahead, for it would give them more time to work on the case. As yet they had found nothing.

James visited Faith as often as he could and he was more worried every time he saw her. She was thin and pale. She told him that she could not eat. The food was as good as could be expected in a place like this, but she just couldn't eat it. She was living on milk and coffee.

It was difficult to talk to her through the double glass partition, with the speaking grill so low that they had to bend down whenever they talked.

"This place is awful," she told him. "I never dreamed that such terrible girls and old women existed. They use the foulest language I have ever heard. Some of them are brought in drunk and they begin to curse and rave when the liquor wears off and they get nervous when they crave a drink. Two of the girls are dope fiends and sometimes I'm afraid they'll hurt me or someone else when they get that craving. One of them was taken to some hospital this morning. She kept us awake last night with her screams and cursing."

He tried to say something that would comfort her, but there was little that he could say.

74

"Have you found anything yet?" she asked as she had done often before.

"Not yet, but I'm sure we will soon," he promised. "That detective will come up with something before long."

"But the time is getting short," she said. "I almost wish that they would take me to the hospital. Anything would be better than staying in this awful place."

"You will be in the hospital if you don't eat more," he warned. "I don't want you to get sick, because when you get out of here we're going to get married."

She stared at him with wide eyes and parted lips.

"Do you really mean that or are you just saying that to cheer me?" she asked.

"I mean it," he said smiling.

He wished that he could take her in his arms and kiss those trembling lips and stroke that lovely hair that had felt so soft beneath his touch.

"I thought you said there was no room in your life for marriage," she argued. "I thought you would be going away and then I'd be left all alone."

"I've changed my mind. If you're willing to marry me and take whatever life brings me, I want to have you with me wherever I may have to go. I can't leave you here alone to get into more trouble."

"Oh, Jimmie!" she exclaimed so softly that he could scarcely hear her above the din around them. "You have made me so happy that I believe I can eat again. I won't ever cry again until I can cry in your arms for joy."

The visiting hour was up and everyone had to leave. He watched her go through the door. She turned and threw him a kiss as she passed out of sight, then he went out with the others. He was not as hopeful as he had tried to make her believe, but he determined that he would not give up hope. This all brought back the memory of his father and that unjust sentence. Justice was sometimes blind and many had suffered through mistakes and failures to discover the truth. He hoped that this would not be another miscarriage of justice.

Finally the day for the trial arrived and neither the

lawyer nor the detective had discovered anything to help them win their case. James was frantic, but he could do nothing but wait and hope, and hope was dim. He had never known the sustaining power of prayer, so he had no strength beyond his own feeble strength upon which to lean in this trying time. He could not eat and he also was losing weight. He tried to concentrate upon his work, but he found it difficult and he made mistakes which he would never have made otherwise.

When the case finally came up for trial it was short and decisive. The prosecution bore down upon Faith unmercifully in an effort to trap her into a confession. Her lawyer did what he could to defend her, but since he had little to go on he knew what the verdict would be before he had finished his defense. She was at the mercy of the court and she was sentenced to eighteen months in prison.

The bookkeeper testified that he had seen Faith slip a small package into her coat the night before she was arrested. The theft was not discovered until the next morning. The prosecution had implied that she had had a confederate who had hidden the stolen goods. Her lawyer had succeeded in having that implication taken from the record, but still it had gone against her in the mind of the judge.

She had maintained her innocence even under the severe grilling the prosecution had put her through. When she heard the verdict she sank back in her chair, a white, crumpled little figure of despair and James feared that she was going to faint.

The matron came and took her back to her cell and left him stunned and raging against a fate that was cruel and unjust, and a justice that could be so blind.

"This may not be the end," Mr. Sutton told him, trying to give him some hope. "Now that she is convicted, whoever stole that jewelry will feel free and he may betray himself. I have an idea that may work. I couldn't have done it before, but now I can."

"What is it?" James asked.

He was not too interested. He felt that the worst had happened and that he would have to go through the same thing that he had lived through before. He would see someone he loved suffer for a crime she did not commit. He felt that Faith would wilt and get sick if she were taken to Angola. If she were sent there he would see her seldom, for the trip was long and he could not take time off from his work. He had spent so much money on the wasted services of that detective and for the lawyer that he could not endanger his job. He must keep that at all hazards.

The days would stretch out endlessly and there would be no ray of sunshine in his life until she was free again. He did not know how to pray for patience and for hope. He knew that if he ever found the man he was searching for, he could do nothing until Faith was out of prison. Just now he didn't care whether he ever found his man. All he wanted was Faith and she would be far away. The future looked hopeless indeed.

CHAPTER **11**

FAITH WAS TRANSFERRED to Angola, the state prison, before James was able to get back to see her. She begged for permission to phone him before she left, but since he was not a relative, she was not allowed to phone. When James went to see her at visiting time, he was told that she was not there. He went to the warden and angrily demanded to know why he was not notified or given the chance to see her before she was taken away. The warden informed him coldly that they had not time to give notice to every boy friend of every prisoner who was sent away.

He left the prison seething with impotent wrath and plunged into the depths of gloom. He determined to try to see her during the weekend and he went to Sutton's office to get his advice and help. He did not know the procedure for arranging to see a prisoner at Angola. He asked the lawyer if he had made any progress in Faith's case and once more asked him to tell what he planned to do.

"I don't want to give you any false hope," Sutton said, "so I cannot tell you what my plan is. I may be entirely wrong, but I have an idea that I am going to follow up. I'll let you know as soon as I can."

James had to be content with that. He took the bus on

Saturday and went to Angola, hoping to be able to see Faith. He took more of her clothes that the landlady had packed for him and he also took a box of candy.

The women's section of the prison was a desolate looking, unattractive place. Several old buildings were surrounded by a high wire fence. In the enclosure there were a few trees, but the place looked neglected and shabby.

The women were allowed in the yard and they were scattered about in groups. Faith was not in sight, but someone went for her. While he waited he had a chance to look about him at the prisoners. For the most part, they were a sodden, hardened-looking lot. There were one or two who looked as if they might be first offenders. They were young girls and he felt pity for them, for he knew that life would never be the same for them after an experience like this. He wondered if anyone else there was as innocent as he knew Faith to be. His whole soul sickened when he thought that if Sutton did not succeed in getting her free she would be in this terrible place more than a year. He didn't believe that she could live through it.

When he saw her coming toward him, he was shocked at the change in her even in this short time. She was ghastly, with dark circles under her eyes and lips as pale as her face. But even so, she looked like a frail lovely flower in an abandoned field of weeds.

He held out his arms to her and she came to him and hid her face against his breast while she sobbed convulsively. Unmindful of the curious stares of the others, he stroked her hair and whispered encouragement to her.

"Don't cry, darling. We have so little time to be together I want to see you smile, not cry. I love you. Doesn't that mean anything to you?"

"Nothing means anything any more," she sobbed. "Why did this have to happen to me? Why did God let it happen? He knows I'm innocent."

It was the same cry that many others had uttered through the years, many who never gave God a thought until they were in trouble, but who blamed Him for not protecting them

79

from harm when they had no right to claim or expect anything from Him.

In this dark hour Faith did not stop to think of the times in the past when her mother had tried hard and prayed desperately for her salvation and she had turned a deaf ear to her mother's plea for her to accept Christ as her Saviour. Now when she lacked the strength and comfort that she so sorely needed, she did not even realize that, perhaps, if she lived in the will of the Lord, this might never have happened. She did not even reproach herself for her indifference to God in the past. She was too intent upon blaming Him for this trouble that had come to her because He had let it happen.

James had no answer to her question. He just held her close and whispered once more that he loved her.

"I'll die if I have to stay here in this place long," she told him as she wiped her eyes and raised her head. "It's terrible here. These prisoners are even worse than those back there in jail. Some of them are here for life and they are terrible. The girl I'm bunking with killed a man and got off with life. She acts sometimes as if she could kill me when she gets in one of her tantrums. The others say they think she is crazy. I'm afraid, Jimmie. Have you done anything to get me out? Isn't my lawyer trying to do something to find the one who really stole that jewelry?"

"He's working on the case, darling. He's doing all he can, but it takes time. Just try to be patient a little longer and I know you'll be out. Then we'll go away somewhere and start a new life together."

"You wouldn't want to marry someone who's been in prison," she said dolefully. "I don't see how you could want to."

"You ought to see. I love you and I know you didn't commit that crime. I love you enough to want to see you happy again."

"I don't think I'll ever be happy again." The tears began to slip from her eyes again.

He wiped them away as he led her to a bench nearby. He gave her the clothes he had brought and the candy. Both packages as well as his person had been searched before he was allowed to leave the entrance office and the clothes were slightly mussed.

"They're not particular how they handle things when they search a person," he remarked. "I was afraid they were going to take that box of candy away from me, for fear that it might contain dope. It was a good thing that it was still sealed. They're mighty particular about some things," he remarked bitterly, forgetting that he was trying to comfort her.

The injustice of this whole affair bit into his soul and added to the bitterness he had carried in his heart for years. He hastened to say something that would drive away the cloud that had spread over her face at his thoughtless words.

"Mrs. Thomas says that she will give us her very best room when we are married," he said. "And at no extra cost. But we won't be staying there too long. We'll get away somewhere far from here, where you'll forget everything that ever happened here."

She shook her head slowly. "I shall never forget it. I shall feel the shame of this the rest of my life. Nothing will ever be the same."

They sat talking until he was forced to leave in order to catch the bus for his return trip.

"I'll come back just as soon as I can," he told her as he held her in his arms. "When I come back, I'm sure that I shall have good news, perhaps an acquittal and some compensation for a false arrest and conviction."

"That would be too good to be true," she said as he kissed her.

She tried to smile as he waved to her when the guard opened the gate to let him out, but she tried in vain. The smile just would not come. She looked at him as if she were seeing him for the last time and swift pain pierced his heart as he turned away and started down the long dusty road that led to the gate. Hope was dim within him as he finally boarded the bus. He realized as he had never done before how his mother must have felt each time she went to see his father, how desolate and hopeless she must have felt, for she did not have the possibility that one day he might be free. Only the long years of a life imprisonment stretched before them. And it had finally killed them both.

Now he was experiencing the same terrible suffering even though there was hope, however faint, that one day soon Faith would be free.

Weeks passed and he heard nothing from Sutton except that he was pursuing the case and that he had hopes of success. Mr. Sutton knew that it was best for James to know nothing about what he was doing, for he did not want any possibility of a slip that would ruin his plan. He realized that if his suspicions were correct, he was dealing with a cunning criminal, one who would be out of his reach if he suspected that anyone was on his trail. As long as he felt that he was not under suspicion, he might betray himself and it was proof that Sutton wanted, not just suspicion.

As time passed and James waited impatiently for some development in the case, he felt so helpless and nervous and impatient that he found it difficult to concentrate upon his work. He knew that it would be disastrous if he should lose his job because of inefficiency. He had been under heavy expense and he had not yet paid all the bills. Mr. Sutton had taken nothing but the contingency fee and he had made it possible for James to pay the detective agency on the installment plan. It would take him a long time to get out of debt and there would be likely be more bills for further detective work. Mr. Sutton had told him that much.

The hate which he had held in his heart for Martin all these years now had an added object. It was the one who had stolen the jewelry. He felt that he could kill the one who had made Faith suffer for his crime. Bitterness and hate raged through him day and night in a maelstrom of emotions. He raged at the injustice of the law, at the inability of the law to detect truth when it was so evident to him, at the heartlessness with which the prosecution bore down upon an innocent victim. He did not stop to think that the law was subject to human weakness and failures, that it was not perfect and that it was the duty of the prosecution to do all in its power to bring a criminal to justice, even though that justice might be mistaken justice. The only thought he had was that he had been one of the victims of mistaken justice and that he had been made to suffer a second time from those mistakes.

Faith wrote to him occasionally as she had promised to do and he wrote to her regularly, but their letters were unsatisfactory for they knew that they were censored, so they could say little about the thing that was uppermost in their thoughts. He could only tell her not to give up hope, that everything would be all right soon. She wrote only a few lines to let him know that she was well and that she was trying to be brave and that she longed to see him again.

He wondered if she told the truth about being well, for she had looked really ill the last time he had seen her and he was worried about her. That little cough she had, had not left her since her cold and, though she did not seem to notice it, it worried him. He remembered his mother, how she had gone down so imperceptibly that he had not realized she was ill until she had a hemorrhage and had to be taken to the hospital.

Spring came after the Mardi Gras season, with its crowds of visitors and the colorful parades and the day of masking. Then the long season of Lent came when the churches were filled with those who believed that a season of penance would atone for the gay and careless lives they had led for many months. They either forgot or they did not know that penance would not atone for their sins, but that the blood of Jesus that was shed on Calvary was the only means of atonement, that faith in Him and acceptance of the gift of salvation through confession to Him that they needed forgiveness and cleansing, was the only means of salvation.

Easter week dawned bright and warm and cloudless. The stores were thronged once more with shoppers buying new outfits and presents for children who would be eagerly searching on the weekend for bright-hued eggs in hidden places.

James was down in the depths. He had not heard from

Faith in several days and he was worried about her. He had not heard from Sutton either. He had dogged his footsteps so often that he had decided not to bother him any more, but to try to wait when waiting was agony.

He had planned to go to see Faith over the weekend, for many business offices would be closed on Good Friday, but he was told that there would be no holiday for his company and that they would work on Saturday also. Business had picked up so that the office was behind with the work. He thought at first that he would go anyway, that he would just not arrive at work, but he decided that this would be too risky, for he might lose his job if he did that. Then he really would be in trouble. He looked forward to a dismally unhappy weekend.

On Monday morning Sutton phoned him and he rushed to the lawyer's office at his lunch hour, too excited to think of eating.

"I think I've found our man," he told James. "I can't be positive; that is, I don't have proof yet, but I think I will have soon. I just want to give you something to hope for because I know what a strain this must have been to you."

"You don't know the half," James said with a sigh. "Who is the man? That bookkeeper?"

"Don't ask any questions," Sutton advised. "I'm hoping to come up with something in just a few days. In the meantime just keep mum and don't act any different from the way you've been acting. You may be watched and if our man gets suspicious, he may skip out and leave us without any proof of his guilt. Then all our work would be for nothing."

"I'll do my best," James promised, "but I don't see how I can live through the days until you do nab him."

He went away from Sutton's office feeling that he had suddenly been released from the torture chamber, but wondering how he could live until he knew for sure that Sutton had his man and his proof.

CHAPTER 12

MR. SUTTON HAD HAD to proceed cautiously with his investigation, for he knew that if the man he suspected once became frightened he would skip out and all would end in failure.

He felt convinced that the bookkeeper was not the guilty one. He and James knew that that ring in Faith's coat was a plant, but they had no proof that it was and the court did not recognize his argument as proof. He was sure that the thief would feel certain that he was safe and as time passed and he saw no indications that he was suspected, he would feel free to carry out any plan he might have had for disposing of the stolen goods and might show his hand and betray himself.

Sutton began to suspect the real culprit when business went on as usual at the shop. Rogers had told James that if he had to pay the owner for the loss, he would be ruined, yet seemingly he had not been affected by the loss. After waiting a reasonable time, Sutton began his search for the insurance company which had insured Rogers. He had no idea which insurance company Rogers had used. He only had the man's statement that his policy had expired.

He proceeded with caution, even in investigating the insurance companies, for fear that his investigation would leak out and Rogers would be warned. After visiting several firms, he at last found the one for which he was searching. They had insured Rogers for a high figure against burglary. The premium was high, but it had been paid regularly each year until this last when Rogers had asked for a deferred payment plan which they had granted. The last payment had been made a short time before the robbery. After the trial they had paid the amount which his inventory showed as the price he had put on the jewelry when he had received it.

Sutton left much encouraged. Rogers had lied about the policy having lapsed. He had a conference with the local head of the insurance company and they agreed to put a special investigator on the case to work with him. Sutton next went to see the owner of the jewelry. Her son met him and told him that his mother had died a short time before the robbery.

"I have just returned from Europe to settle my mother's estate," he told Sutton. "I was ill when she died and couldn't get here until now."

When Sutton told him of the transaction regarding the jewelry, he was amazed and angry.

"My mother sold him that jewelry. He didn't take it on consignment. I came across the receipt for it just yesterday. She must have been out of her mind to have let that fellow have it. I don't know what kind of persuasion he used, but he surely tricked her if she let him have it for that amount. She should have taken those pieces to a reputable jeweler and not to that shop. They were antiques that were really worth a fortune. I shall look into this as soon as I can."

"Please don't do anything yet," Sutton advised. "I have an investigator on the case and if we succeed in our plans, we shall nab the criminal and get the jewelry back. If you do anything now, you may frighten him and we will lose our man and you will lose your jewelry."

Rogers had evidently forged papers covering the transaction after the owner had died, increasing the amount he had actually paid. Her death had given him the chance to steal the jewelry and collect the insurance. He had had to show the papers covering the transaction to the insurance company before they would pay for the loss. Their one mistake was in not contacting the owner of the jewelry before they paid for the loss. However, Sutton explained to them that it would not have helped since the owner was dead.

All of this information still did not give enough proof that he had stolen the jewelry and collected on the insurance. They would have to get further proof before he could be arrested.

Investigation of Rogers' checking account revealed nothing. He was too astute for that. Evidently he had the money hidden somewhere and, at the proper time, when he was sure that no suspicion rested upon him, he would skip out with the money and the jewelry.

This was just what he tried to do. He proceeded in a cautious, legal, orderly way. He offered his business for sale. When he was approached by a prospective buyer, who was the insurance investigator, and this person asked him why he was selling out, he told the man with apparent frankness, that a recent robbery had put him so deeply in the red that he was giving up in disgust. He said that the business had been and was still good, but that he was in bad health and did not have the strength to carry on while trying to pay for the lost jewelry.

The buyer still appeared interested and asked if he might have an inventory of the stock and a look at the books. Without hesitation Rogers consented. He did not know that this man was a skilled accountant and could detect fraudulent accounts. The inventory and a seemingly careless auditing of the books revealed to the investigator that the business was on the verge of bankruptcy. Much of the stock was held on consignment and there were unpaid bills which the stock could not possibly cover. However, on the surface everything pointed to a profitable business. The investigator wondered how much the wizened bookkeeper knew about this, whether he was not in this as deep as his employer.

He finally said that he would buy the business, but that he would have to make arrangements for a loan and get a complete appraisal of the stock. He promised to be back in a day or so and sign the necessary papers. On the night before the buyer was to phone him that he would return to sign the final papers, Rogers was arrested on his way to the bus depot. In his suitcase was all the stolen jewelry as well as the money from the insurance company.

Sutton phoned James the next morning and he went to Sutton's office at once.

"We have our man," he told James. "It was Rogers. And he had everything in his possession. In no time at all our little girl will be given a full acquittal. I don't know what they will do to atone for this miscarriage of justice, perhaps nothing. The main thing is that she will be free and that your worries will be over."

"They ought to be made to pay for all the suffering they have caused her," James declared. "I'd like to beat that prosecuting lawyer to a pulp for the way he grilled her. He was such a brute."

"Don't do anything that will get you into more trouble," Sutton warned. "It is his duty to get a conviction for every prisoner brought before the court."

"It's the duty of the law to believe a person innocent until he's proved to be guilty, but what that court did was to prove her guilty and never give her a chance to prove her innocence."

"That's one of the tragedies we have to face in this business," Sutton told him. "No one is infallible and this only proves that the law is not, either."

"But I've gone through this a second time now," James remarked harshly. "I hate the whole rotten system. I don't believe they know what justice is."

"I'm sorry. I didn't know," Sutton replied sympathetically.

James regretted his thoughtless words. He had never mentioned his past experience to anyone before and he did not want anyone to know this for it might be dangerous to him in the future.

"It happened a long time ago," he explained. "Someone I knew was jailed for something he didn't do. He was set free when the law found out that it had made a mistake."

He hoped that this lie would take Sutton's mind off of what he had let slip.

"Nothing matters now but that Faith will be free. How long will it take to get her out of that awful place?" he asked.

"Not long, I'm sure. Of course there is some red tape, but that ought not to take long. We'll get her out with full exoneration as soon as possible."

James took the night bus to St. Francisville and went to the prison the next day. He had an order allowing him to see Faith even though it was not a regular visiting day. He was told that she was in the hospital. His fears were realized and he got there as quickly as he could.

When he saw her he was more shocked than he had been on that first visit to the prison. Her eyes were bright with fever and her face was flushed, but she was so thin that he imagined he could see the bones beneath her fair skin. Her hands on the sheet looked so frail that he was almost afraid to touch them.

"Jimmie!" she cried weakly as he came and stood by the bed. "I was wishing for you. How glad I am that you are here! I can't take it here much longer." Her lips trembled though she tried to keep her voice steady.

"You're not going to have to take it any longer, my darling," he told her as he sat down by the bed and took one small hand in both of his. He bent and kissed her forehead. "You've suffered too much already. They found the real thief and you will be set free in a few days, exonerated from the charge."

"Was it the bookkeeper?"

"No. It was Rogers. I can't understand why they didn't suspect him in the beginning. I can't understand why that insurance company didn't put their investigator on the case. They were so sure that you were the guilty one that they didn't bother to go into the case with any real interest. If that fellow ever gets out of prison and I can get my hands on him, I'll take care of him."

"That wouldn't undo what's been done," she warned. "How soon can I get out of here?"

"Sutton said it would take a day or so, but just as soon as I can get to town and get an ambulance, I'll have you taken back. They owe you that much and I'm going to see that they send for you at once."

He noticed her short breathing and that her cough was worse than when he had seen her last and cold fear gripped him. He remembered his mother's symptoms and he sickened when he thought of what had followed. He had not known then what he knew now and he had not paid too much attention until he knew the worst, but now he saw those same symptoms. He tried to encourage himself as he sat looking at her. Perhaps this was just the result of what she had been through, the shock, the despair and the lack of food. When he could get her back where he could give her everything she needed and she was happy again, these symptoms would disappear. His heart was heavy with foreboding, however, when he left her and returned to the city.

He went at once to see Sutton and told him what he had found. Sutton got an immediate interview with the district attorney. James went with him and, in spite of Sutton's warning and his promise to say nothing, his wrath exploded when he met with the district attorney's seeming indifference to the situation.

"Of course I'm sorry that this had to happen," he said, "but sometimes we do make mistakes."

"You're sorry the court made a mistake!" James exploded. "It was you and it was a stupid miscarriage of justice. It was all your fault and if that innocent girl dies, you will be her murderer. Yet you sit there calmly and say that you're sorry! You should have taken the time to look into the case instead of jumping at conclusions and sending her off to prison to get sick and perhaps die."

The district attorney eyed him coldly.

"This interview is between your lawyer and myself. Will you step into the next room until we have finished?"

He rang a buzzer and James was escorted into the

waiting room while Sutton and the district attorney finished their business.

When Sutton came out he gave James a look of disapproval.

"That was a foolish thing to do," he said. "It didn't do any good. You promised not to say anything."

"I'm sorry," James apologized, "but I lost my head when I thought of what his mistake has meant to Faith. Did he agree to see that she is sent back at once?"

"Yes, he said that he would have an ambulance sent for her. Her acquittal has already been signed."

"A signed acquittal!" James exclaimed wrathfully. "That is all she gets in return for what they have made her suffer."

"Try not to be so bitter," Sutton urged. "It won't help matters and the best thing you can do is try to forget what has happened and to be happy now that you two can be together again. Holding such vindictiveness in your heart will only keep you from being happy."

"I never expect to forget it," James retorted. "It's easy to say forget, but if you've ever tried it, you know that it's impossible. Not something like this. I want to go up there with that ambulance."

"I'll see if it can be arranged," Sutton promised.

"There's no question about seeing whether it can be arranged. I'm going. They owe me that much. They should be sued for false imprisonment."

"That would be hard to do, so don't think of trying it," Sutton advised.

When James returned to work his face was like a storm cloud. The others in the office wondered what had happened. They knew, of course, about the trial. Finally one of them asked him if he was in more trouble.

"Yes, plenty," he replied. "They're bringing my girl home in an ambulance. She's sick. That rotten court has just about killed her. I'd like to tear every one of them apart, from the judge on down, everyone who had anything to do with sending her to prison."

They offered their sympathy. They could understand how he felt, but they did not respond to his outburst of bitterness and fury.

He made the trip to Angola with the ambulance and came back sitting beside Faith. They made the trip for the most part in silence. He did not want to tax her strength by letting her talk.

When they reached the rooming house, she gave him a smile and whispered, "It will be good to be at home again and to know that I'm free at last."

They carried her gently upstairs to her room and Mrs. Thomas hovered near, willing to do anything that would make her more comfortable.

"I'll bring you some good soup that I've just made, she offered. "You'll need to get fattened up and get your strength back."

"I shall feel like eating now," Faith told her and gave her a feeble smile.

"I think we'd better get a doctor first and see what he says," James suggested.

He phoned Sutton and asked him to recommend a good doctor. He gave James the name of his own physician and offered to phone the doctor himself. It was not long before the doctor arrived.

His face was serious as he examined Faith and James' heart sank lower into the depths as he watched the long and thorough examination and listened to the doctor's questions. Finally he turned to James.

"I hate to tell you this, but I am pretty sure that she has a cavity in one lung."

James looked at him as if he had just received the death sentence for himself. Faith did not hear what was said, but she could tell by the look on James' face that the news was not good.

"What is it, Jimmie?" she asked. "I want to know."

James hesitated. He did not want to frighten her, but the doctor whispered, "She will have to know, so you had better let me tell if you don't want to."

James nodded and the doctor turned to her and explained her condition as encouragingly as he could.

"You have a little cavity in one of those lungs that must be filled up. That is why you have that cough that keeps hanging on. We'll get you to a hospital and get to work on you so that you'll be well again. Just keep as quiet as you can and eat all the good food you can. And drink lots of milk."

James followed him into the hall.

"What shall I do?" he asked.

"I'll make arrangements for her to be admitted to the Dibert Memorial Building. That is where tuberculosis patients are kept. She will get the best of attention there and it won't cost you anything. I'll look in on her and do everything I can to help her get well."

"How long do you think it will take?" James asked tensely.

"That's hard to say," the doctor replied. "Much depends upon her response to the treatment and upon the extent of the cavity. X-rays will determine that. It may take six months or a year or longer. I can't tell you any more than that."

James thanked him as he left, then he went back to Faith.

"The doctor didn't fool me with that baby talk," she told him. "I have tuberculosis. I'm afraid, Jimmie! So afraid! It's a terrible disease. I know I'll never get well. Oh, Jim, why did it have to be this way? Why did God let this happen to me?"

Once more, in the face of terror and despair, she failed to remember that she had no claim upon God nor any right to question Him. Even now she did not remember all the years past when she had had every opportunity to become God's child and to come within His arc of safety, where she would have had strength and faith enough to meet every testing wihout fear, knowing that she was safe in Him, no matter what might come.

James knelt by the bed and put his arms around her and held her close. He put his cheek against hers which was so hot with fever and murmured endearments to her.

"You're going to get well, darling. God won't let you die. He can't! I need you and we're going to get married and we'll live happily out west somewhere where you can get strong and well again. I want to marry you right away, little one, so that I can give you all the attention you will need."

She stroked his head with her thin hand and smiled tenderly into his adoring eyes.

"I can't marry you until I'm well again. It wouldn't be fair to you. I wouldn't want to be a burden to you any more than I have been. I've been a burden and a worry to you ever since we first met. And I did so want to make you happy."

"You do make me happy by just loving me," he said and kissed her on her cheek. "We'll argue about getting married when you're a little stronger. Here is Mrs. Thomas with some soup. Eat a lot, for it will do you good."

"I'm sure that this will help you feel better," Mrs. Thomas remarked as she set a little bed tray before Faith and helped to prop her up with pillows.

"Now I think you should try to get some sleep," James told her when she had finished.

"I shall try. I'm tired," she admitted. "That soup was the best food I've had since I left here," and she gave Mrs. Thomas a smile. "Thank you."

They left her and James went to his room and threw himself on the bed. It was still early but he felt exhausted. The shock of knowing Faith's condition had left him weak and utterly spent. It seemed more than he could stand. Just one misfortune after another and now this. What next, he wondered. He turned his face to the wall and tried not to think, for thinking only made him more miserable. Finally he slept, but his dreams were mixed up dreams of horror and he wakened without feeling refreshed.

He went to see Faith but the doctor had left something to make her sleep and she had not wakened. He went back to his room and undressed. The night was long and he spent hours in sleepless tossing while his thoughts whirled in a rebellious storm against this blow that fate had dealt him. In this dark hour he could not reach out from the darkness to the One who could have given him peace, so in his heart there was nothing but fear and wretchedness while he fought off despair.

CHAPTER 13

THE NEXT DAY Faith was taken to the Dibert Memorial Building. James followed the ambulance and waited nervously while she was being checked in and assigned to her ward. It was a long and tedious time of waiting, for there were many other patients ahead of her with other ailments.

It was with mingled emotions that he followed the roller which took her across the covered walk to the Dibert Building and up to her bed in the observation ward. It brought back many memories of the last time he had been in such a building, the rows of white beds, the patients in various stages of illness. Some of them were able to be propped up and were reading or crocheting, some were too ill to sit up or even talk. All of them were waiting as patiently as they could for the result of tests and the verdict which would either give them hope that they would be able to recover with only bed rest or whether they would have to undergo the torturing experience of taking air so that the lung might be collapsed slowly in order to have rest and a better chance of healing.

There were so many new drugs which had given encouraging results that the terror which had filled the hearts of those condemned to hospitalization was removed in a large measure and hope had taken the place of despair and hopelessness.

For a little while after she was finally put in the bed she would occupy until the tedious rounds of tests should be completed, Faith closed her eyes and lay resting. She was exhausted by the ambulance ride, the long wait in the admission room and the trip across to the Dibert Building, with the added strain of anxiety and fear. She had never been in a large hospital before and the sight of the other patients in long rows terrified her. They made her more aware of her condition and made her feel that she was no longer an individual with a personality. She was just another case. James would be restricted to visiting hours and those hours were short.

When she opened her eyes she saw him sitting beside her, looking at her with adoring, pain-filled gaze. A nurse was just approaching to take her temperature and count her pulse, so for a few minutes she could do nothing but return his look while her heart cried out to him of her love and her terror.

When the nurse finally left to go down the line with her thermometers in small glasses of germicide, James leaned over and whispered words of encouragement. Tears filled her eyes in spite of her effort to restrain them.

"I wonder how long they will keep me here," she said. "Have you any idea? What did the doctor say?"

"He said he didn't know. They will have to take X-rays and make other tests to find out what your condition is. You may not be here long. Let's hope that you won't."

Neither of them thought of praying that the time would not be long. Perhaps it was best that they did not, for they did not know, though Faith should have known, that they could not call upon God to answer such a prayer if they did not belong to Him as His children.

"I'm afraid I'm going to be here a long time," she sighed. "I know I'm mighty sick. I felt this coming on for quite a while, but I didn't want to give way to it. I kept hoping that I'd get better."

"You should have had a doctor before now," he said.

"If you had, you might be well by now. But it's too late to think of what might have been. Let's just try to be happy and look forward to the time when we can be married."

He gave her a smile of encouragement, but there was no answering smile upon her lips. Just then an intern came in with his chart and sat by her and began to ask questions. James wondered why, when the visiting hour was so short, they had to take a time like this to interfere with a visit which meant much to both the patient and the visitor.

While he sat impatiently waiting for the intern to leave, his eyes wandered to the patients in the other beds. Just opposite Faith's bed there was a patient who looked even younger than Faith. She was propped by pillows and had a book open before her. By her side sat a young girl, perhaps in her early twenties, who was talking to her and pointing out passages in the book. His attention was arrested as he watched this visitor. She was strikingly pretty, with dark hair cut short and framing her face with ringlets. He could hear her voice, low and melodious, though he could not hear what she was saying.

He looked at the patient who was listening with such absorbed interest to what the visitor was saying. She smiled at some remark and he noticed how radiant she seemed. There was a look of peace upon her face, even though she was thin and pale. He contrasted this peace with the look of fear and hopelessness upon Faith's face as she answered the intern's questions and let him use his stethoscope.

The visiting girl glanced for a moment at him and then at Faith. In that one swift glance James noted that she was even more lovely when he could look into her dark eyes than she was in profile. Her lips were firm and red and her brows were dark and straight, but there was a dimple in her chin which gave a cherubic aspect to a face which might otherwise have been too strong for perfect feminine beauty. The look that she fastened upon Faith was so full of compassion that he felt his own heart melt beneath its glance. It was so filled with love and sympathy that he felt the tears sting his eyes even though he was ashamed of this momentary weakness. She seemed to understand just what Faith was suffering, the fear that possessed her and the pain he was bearing.

He wished that he could talk to her, for he somehow felt that if he could she might impart to Faith some of the peace and strength which she seemed to possess. She turned back to the patient and what had been only an instant had seemed much longer to him because of the emotions which that one brief glance had aroused within him. While the intern continued his endless examination, he could not take his eyes off the scene before him. Finally the girl closed the book and both of them bowed their heads. He heard the murmur of the girl's mellow voice and he knew that she was praying. He could never remember praying and he felt that he was intruding by even watching as she prayed.

When she finished, there were tears in the eyes of the young patient, but there was a smile upon her face, a smile of happiness which he couldn't understand. Then the young visitor rose and took the book. As she passed him, their eyes met again, but her glance passed over him to Faith and she gave her a warm smile. Faith, to his surprise, answered that smile with her own, something which he had not been able to coax from her unwilling lips. As she passed, James saw that the book was the Bible. It seemed incongruous to him that those two young people should be interested in reading it. He had never even thought of reading it. In fact, he could not remember ever having looked inside one. There had been one in his home, but he had never seen his mother reading it nor had his father ever opened it. But these two girls had seemed interested.

He glanced once more at the patient and he noticed that she had opened her own Bible and was marking certain passages in it. She looked up and saw him watching her and she gave him a friendly smile. He felt embarrassed because she had caught him staring at her and he turned his attention to Faith. The intern was just leaving and he was thankful, for his time was almost up.

"You'd think I was going to be here forever, by the questions he asked and the time he took," Faith said wearily.

"I don't see how I can stay in this place for long." She turned her tearful eyes to him. "I'll be lonesome, Jimmie. This is almost like being back in prison."

"You know it isn't," he protested, taking her hand and holding it tenderly. "You'll have me with you a little while every day and you'll have these patients in this ward instead of those low characters who were in prison. And you'll be getting better every day. I think that young girl over there opposite you will be good for you to have as a friend. See how happy she looks. You'd think she didn't have a worry in the world."

"Perhaps she's almost well," Faith replied skeptically.

She couldn't see how anyone could be happy in this place with the terrible disease she had.

"She doesn't look like it," he argued. "She looks sicker than you."

Just then the girl felt their gaze upon her and raised her eyes to meet theirs. She smiled at Faith and waved a hand at her. James saw how thin that hand was. Surely, physically, she had little to make her look happy and contented. It must have been the contact with that lovely young girl. He wished that Faith might have that girl as a visitor, if she could do for her what she had done for this girl. Faith waved back to her and just then the bell rang, a signal for all visitors to leave.

James leaned over and kissed Faith on her forehead.

"I'll be back this evening," he told her. "Be good and try to get some sleep. Remember that rest and sleep will do more than anything else to get you well fast."

She managed a smile as he left her, but his heart was heavy. He felt more lonely than he had felt since his mother had waved to him for the last time and had given him a similar wan smile.

CHAPTER 14

WHEN JAMES FINALLY got to bed after that first trying day with Faith at the hospital, he dropped off to sleep without any delay. He was mentally and physically exhausted. He was worried about Faith and worried about the bills to be paid, about which Faith knew nothing. He had used up almost all of the money he had and he knew that it would be a long time before he would be out of debt. He did not know what Faith might need in the future. He wanted her to have everything possible to help her get well and to take care of her when she was discharged from the hospital.

He went about his work in a fog of misery and despondency. He was tortured by mingled emotions hate and the desire for revenge, fear and worry over Faith and her condition, and desperation when he thought of himself and what the future might hold for him.

His hands were tied for the present, as far as finding the man for whom he had come to search. It gave him a sense of frustration, for he was forced to give up the search for the present and he might be forced to give it up forever. His only free time would be taken up with his visits to the hospital. He went there from one to two and from six to seven each day. The only time he would have to look for his man would be on

Sunday and he knew that he couldn't go to a man's home on the pretext of business on a Sunday. He had exchanged his lunch hour with another employee who had a one o'clock hour so that he could see Faith then.

When she was discharged, and that seemed to be a long time in the future, if he married her he could not carry out his plan for murder. He had to confess the truth to himself that this wild scheme for revenge was just plain murder. If he married her he would have to take her somewhere out west where the climate would be more suitable for her, and a fugitive from the law could not pick and choose his place of abode. Even if he found his man while she was still in the hospital he could do nothing about it, for he could not run away and leave her alone. Even if he did not love her so much it would be cruel to leave her alone when she needed him and was helpless and dependent upon him.

He felt that the goal which he had set for himself to avenge his father's and mother's deaths had suddenly eluded him and there seemed to be a great void in his life, as if he had spent his years looking toward something that had suddenly been put out of his reach. He felt that he was failing in his life's purpose and that he was failing them.

He knew that it was not meant for man to take the law into his own hands, but he did not care. He was doggedly determined to make a man pay for the crime he had committed. He was not willing to let God take care of the one who had done this thing, in His own way which was the only perfect way.

He knew nothing of God except that He existed. He believed that and he felt that his mother had also believed, though she had shown little of the fruits of her belief, for she had taught him nothing except vague principles of right and wrong. Even this inadequate teaching had done nothing to eradicate from his heart hate and revenge as his life's purpose.

He did not yet know what Faith's condition was. He had asked the doctor in charge of her case but he had gotten no definite information. He discovered that they gave out little information, except to prepare a patient for taking air or for an operation when that was necessary. Faith had tried to get some information but had met with the same failure. She was told that she would have to wait for further tests and additional X-rays. She learned from the other patients what a long and trying time it was before they were finally classified and either sent to other wards or kept for a further stay in the observation room.

She had become acquainted with the girl in the bed opposite her and this girl had tried to cheer her up and to give her encouragement, but her efforts had met with failure. Faith was still in the depths of despair. The girl in the next bed was sullen and gloomy and complained constantly about everything. Her attitude did not help Faith to become reconciled to her lot. James realized this and was glad when the patient was finally moved to another ward.

When he visited Faith he looked for the girl he had seen that first day visiting the girl opposite but he did not see her again. He was tempted to ask the girl, Jane Price, about her, but thought better of it. She had interested him even though he had been worried and upset, for she seemed to be able to impart peace and he knew that this was something that Faith sorely needed. He did not consider peace for himself, for he felt that peace was not for him. He could not have it until his mission was accomplished and he knew that if it ever was, he could not expect it even then.

One day at the noon hour she came and he learned why she had not been there before. He heard her tell Jane that she had been helping to nurse her father who had been quite ill. James could not resist watching her as the annoying intern came in and made his rounds, interrupting his visit with Faith. He wished that he had the courage to speak to her before she left and to ask her if she would visit Faith, for he was sure that she could pull Faith out of the depths, but he was reluctant to do so for fear that she might resent his speaking to her.

The next day he was so ill that he could not go to work. He tossed and worried through days of high fever and a wracking cough before he finally sent for the doctor. The doctor forbade him to go back to the hospital until the cough had disappeared.

"It will not be safe for either you or Faith," the doctor said. "It would lay you open to infection and if she should take a cold it would be much worse for her."

He promised to let James know how she was and to tell her why he could not come to see her, but that did not keep him from worrying. He tried to phone her but he could get little satisfaction from the ones who answered the phone. Faith, of course, could not come to the phone. He had to be satisfied with the doctor's promise to let her know why he was not there.

The doctor told him the truth about Faith's condition and he warned James not to tell her how serious it was. She would be in the hospital for a long time. The cavity was large and he feared that if she did not respond to treatment, one lobe of the lung would have to be removed. That, of course, would be a serious operation.

James sank to the depths at the news and faced the future with a heavy heart. He was more anxious than ever to see Faith, for he knew that she would need moral strength for the possible ordeal ahead of her. The future looked dark indeed.

It seemed that his cough would never leave and he waited impatiently to be free to visit her again. When he went back after what seemed an eternity to him, he feared that he would find her in the depths. To his surprise she greeted him with a cheerful smile. There were no tears and no despairing wail that he had expected, but a glad cry as she saw him coming through the door.

"Jimmie! How glad I am that you are well again! I've prayed so that you would soon be able to come back again and here you are. How wonderful the Lord has been to let you come back today when I was longing so for you."

Her words gave him a shock and he wondered if she had a fever. He couldn't quite get over the surprise as he sat down and looked at her in puzzled amazement. She put out her hand and he took it in his while he still stared silently at her, at a loss for words.

"You're looking thin and you're still pale," she observed as she scanned his face anxiously. "I was afraid that I might have given you one of my germs. I would never forgive myself if I had."

"It was nothing but a bad cold," he assured her. "The doctor said it was a touch of the flu. It was pretty tough, though," he added. "Knocked me out completely."

"It seemed ages to me while you were away. If it hadn't been for the peace I've had in my heart, I don't think I could have stood it. I would have been crying all the time, especially when you just disappeared without a word."

"I was too sick to even try to phone you until I finally sent for the doctor," he told her.

He continued to stare at her, puzzled at the miraculous change in her. He wondered if it was the effect of some of the new drugs they were giving her.

"Something wonderful has happened to me since you were here," she said as he continued silent. "It was a miracle from the Lord."

"Tell me about it." Truly some miracle had happened to her.

"At last I've come to the Lord," she told him. Her voice was low, but there was such quiet happiness in it that he marveled. "I've accepted Christ as my Saviour. After all these years when I was so indifferent and rebellious, I wonder how God could forgive me and save me, but He did, and I've never had such peace and joy in my heart, in spite of this illness, in all my life."

He was still mystified, but he was interested in anything that would bring that look of peace to her and keep her tears from pouring forth. She really had come out of the depths and he knew that it had nothing to do with her physical condition.

"Tell me about it," he urged. "How did it happen?"

"It all came about through Jane," she told him. "Just before she was moved to another ward she had a visitor, a

Miss Martinez. I saw them talking and both of them looked so happy as they read from some book that I wished she would come and talk to me. When she was on her way out, she gave me a smile and I suppose she must have seen the longing in my eyes, for she stopped and spoke to me. She said afterwards that it was the Lord who had impelled her to stop. She asked if she could talk to me for a little while and I was so lonesome that I was glad to talk to anyone. Then she began to talk to me about Christ. She asked me if I were saved, if I had ever confessed to the Lord that I was a sinner and asked Him to forgive me and save my soul and I had to tell her the truth, that I never had. Then she began to talk to me just as my mother used to talk. I felt guilty when I thought of Mother and how indifferent I had been to her pleadings.''

Her voice trembled and her eyes misted for a moment and she hesitated, trying to steady her voice, then she continued.

"She told me that all these years the Lord had been patiently waiting for me to open the door of my heart and let Him come in and bring peace and hope. She told me how easy it was to let Him in, that all I had to do was to want Him to come in and that if I did and if I asked Him, that the blood of the Lord Jesus would cleanse all my sin and that there would be peace in my heart such as I had never known. While she talked to me I wanted to ask the Lord to forgive me and I told her so. She prayed with me and I prayed just what she told me to pray. I told the Lord that I knew I was a sinner and that I wanted Him to forgive me and save me. And then He did. It was wonderful, Jimmie!''

He nodded, though he still couldn't understand.

"At first I wasn't sure, but she told me that when I had asked the Lord to forgive me and save me, I had done all any human being could do, and that He had done it all when He shed His blood on the Cross. She said that if I had done all I could do, then I must believe that God would do what He said He would do, for He had said, 'He that cometh unto me I will in no wise cast out.' Then I knew and I believed and now I know that I'm saved and I'm so happy.''

"I'm glad that you're happy," he whispered. "That makes me happy, too."

"But you'll never be really happy, deep down within your soul, Jimmie, unless you accept Christ as your Saviour as I did. You're precious and I love you, but you're a sinner, too, because the Bible says that all have sinned and come short of the glory of God."

How true it was that he was a sinner! He knew that. Her words brought him face to face with the fact that the hate he had harbored in his heart was sin and the murder he was contemplating was also a sin. He did not know that, according to God's Word he had already committed that crime, for the hate and the desire were there in his heart. He failed to realize that sin was not alone an act, but the impulse or desire which prompted the act. But he did not want to talk about this matter of sin. He couldn't, for the barrier of that hate and his dogged purpose to keep it there until it had brought forth its fruit would stand between him and any possible hope of forgiveness and salvation. He did not want it. Not just now, at least.

"I wish you would get saved, Jimmie," Faith said. "It would make me happy and it would take that dark look off your face that I've seen there so often when you didn't even realize it was there. I don't know what brings it there, but I know that God could take it away so that it would never come back again."

"It's not for me, little one, at least not just now. I've got too many other things on my mind. Let's talk about you. I love you, I love you," he whispered.

"I love you, Jimmie, more than my life," she answered. "That's why I want you to have what I have, because I want the best in life for you."

Their conversation was interrupted by someone who came in and stopped by Faith's bed. James was glad for the interruption. He saw that it was the girl he had seen talking to Jane.

"I'm glad you came just now," Faith said. "We were talking about you."

She introduced them and as James rose to acknowledge the introduction and met her friendly gaze, her brown eyes seemed more lovely than he had thought and she herself was far more attractive when she smiled and her eyes became alight with that smile.

"I've been telling Jimmie what a blessing you've been to me," Faith told her. "Won't you sit down?"

"No. I have another patient down in another ward and I won't interrupt your visit. I'll be back again."

"Isn't she beautiful?" Faith asked when she had gone.

"Yes, she is," he agreed. There was something more than mere physical beauty which shone from her face and radiated like a beam of light from within. "What was her name? I didn't get it."

"Linda Martinez. She comes here almost every day, sometimes during visiting hours and sometimes before the crowd gets here. She visits all the new patients and if they want her to, she reads the Bible with them and helps them to grow after they are saved. She gave me a little Testament and I read it every day. She said she doesn't know how she missed me in the beginning, but I know that it was for the best, for she came just when I needed her most. She said that is how the Lord works. He comes just when we need Him the most."

Just then the bell rang and James had to hurry back to work. He had been late in getting to the hospital and they had not had much time together. When he left Faith, his anxiety about her mental condition was gone. He felt that she would no longer sink to despair and he was deeply grateful to Linda Martinez for what she had done.

They met in the hall while waiting for the elevator and they went down in it alone. On their way out they walked along together.

"I want to thank you for what you did to help Faith," he said. "You've done wonders for her and I'm grateful."

"It was not I who did it. It was the Lord. I was only the instrument in His hands to lead her to Him."

Her face was serious but her eyes glowed as she spoke

and once again he observed how expressive and how lovely they were.

"No matter who it was, it was a miracle," he stated. "I never saw such a change in anyone. The last time I saw her she was in the depths and was crying most of the time. Now she seems happy."

"She is happy," Linda assured him, "and she'll never be afraid again because she has the peace of God in her heart and that takes away all fear."

They reached the lot where her car was parked and she offered to give him a lift. He accepted gladly when she said that she was going downtown. He was in a hurry to get back to work, but he was glad to have the opportunity to be with her a little longer. She had attracted him from the first time he had seen her and he wanted to get better acquainted with her. He felt that he could never forget her for what she had done for Faith.

When she had gotten out into traffic, she turned a brief glance upon him.

"I wonder if you have the peace of God in your heart as Faith has in hers, Mr. Thornton. Have you ever accepted Christ as your Saviour?"

He was surprised and embarrassed by her direct question. He had certainly not expected this. If he had, he never would have gone with her. He had to confess that he had not.

"Faith would be happy if you would and you would be happy yourself. We need strength beyond our own to carry us through in this world, for today it seems that everywhere we turn there is temptation and testing and only those who are strong in the Lord are able to overcome."

The conversation was getting decidedly out of hand. It was most disturbing and he wished that she would change the subject or that he could.

"I've never thought much about it," he confessed.

"I hope that for Faith's sake you will think about it," she said. "She's going to need you more than ever in the weeks to come and if you have God's strength, it will help both of you. I'm afraid that she is in for a trying time."

"How did you know?" he asked in surprise.

"Perhaps I shouldn't have said that," she replied, "but I've seen so many there that I can pretty well judge when a patient has a serious condition. I don't mean to frighten you, but she will need you much in the days ahead. I'm sure that your own physician has told you that her condition is serious."

"Yes, he did, but I thought that she was getting along well."

"She is and I thank the Lord for that, but she thinks she will be out in just a few weeks or a few months. I'm afraid that it will be longer than that. I'm only telling you this to emphasize the fact that you will need a strength that is greater than your own. Please think about it."

They had reached the corner where he had to get out and he left after thanking her again for her interest in Faith.

As she drove away she wondered if she had done the right thing in telling him about Faith's condition. Perhaps she hadn't, but she wanted to do something to jar him out of his stolid indifference. She could tell when someone was interested and willing to listen to the message of salvation and she knew that he was not willing, but stubbornly resisting. She sighed as she drove home. If he could only realize what he was turning away from! Perhaps someday he would see before it was too late. She prayed earnestly that he would.

CHAPTER 15

JAMES MET LINDA FREQUENTLY after this, either in the ward or on their way out. Occasionally he rode with her downtown and he looked forward to this opportunity to be with her. After that first time she had never approached him further about his spiritual condition, but she did make him conscious of the fact by remarks about Faith and the peace and hope she now had and also by telling him some of her experiences with other patients.

She told him about a thrilling experience she had had when she had talked to a patient who had been brought in after a severe hemorrhage. He was a horrible sight, for he was covered with blood and was too weak to be cleaned. He had several days' growth of beard on his face and he was blind in one eye. The eye was still there but it was white and swollen as some injured eyes are.

This man knew nothing about salvation when she slipped into the room where he was alone and asked if she might talk to him. When she began to talk to him and explained what salvation meant, he had been willing to accept the Lord and there were tears streaming down his face when he prayed, but there was a smile upon his lips when she left him. When she went back to see him on her next visit he was a changed person and he greeted her with such a smile that it brought joy to her heart.

"He told his wife about me and from then until the day he died he called me his angel. I think he got the idea from some picture he had seen. It was a joy to talk to him, for he was eager to learn as much as he could about the Bible.

"He was different from many others," she remarked. "Many are indifferent to the fact that they are lost and many others seek to justify themselves by saying that they never harmed anyone and they do all the good they can, while others are just so indifferent that they do not care. They are the ones I grieve over. I pray for them that they may see their danger and their opportunity and that they will remember what I tried to tell them and will get right with God. It will be a terrible thing to fall into the hands of the living God with a soul that has not been cleansed by the blood."

He wondered if she had been praying for him. He hoped that she had, yet he was afraid that she had. How could he ever be saved when he had such plans in his heart and such hatred and vindictiveness there?

Even though her conversation often disturbed him, he was eager to be with her at every opportunity, for when he was with her she seemed to give him a sense of peace. While he listened to her interesting conversation he admired her beauty and her strength of character. She was different from anyone he had ever known.

"I shouldn't bore you with my little personal experiences," she apologized after she had related this experience. "Though they mean much to me, I know they can't mean anything to you, and I'm sure you're not interested."

"But I am," he insisted. "Just to hear you tell them makes them seem wonderful."

His words and his look did not hint of anything but friendship, but she turned her eyes away and faint color suffused her clear skin. When she left him at his corner and drove toward home, there was a frown upon her face and a worried light in her eyes. She set her lips firmly together as the car shot forward at higher speed.

She would not see him again. He belonged to that poor little girl who loved him so much. What right had she to be interested in him except for his soul's salvation? He was good-looking, but she had met other boys who were just as good-looking and boys who were Christians, boys she had known all her life. She knew nothing about this stranger and he was in love with Faith, so why should she be interested in him? She would not see him again. She could not afford to become interested in him in that way. Nevertheless that unconscious look of admiration that he had given her brought a quickening to her heart even while she reproached herself for it.

As time passed Linda found that it was not easy to avoid him. Frequently Faith asked her to wait until he came and begged her to talk to her about the Bible while he was there, so that perhaps he might hear and want to be saved. She was anxious for him to have what she had and this was the only way she could think of to witness to him, for her own feeble efforts had failed miserably.

Linda could not refuse and made it a point to be there occasionally when he came. He would find them talking and would take a chair on the other side of the bed and sit silently while they read and talked. His eyes never left Linda's face and she felt his absorbed gaze and tried not to feel self-conscious as she gave out the Word. She prayed that in some way he might be impressed and that his heart might be opened to the Word. She did not remain long and went to see other patients, but when the bell rang he would be at the elevator waiting for her.

"Could I beg you for a lift?" he asked one afternoon as she was about to leave without offering to take him.

"I'm sorry, but I am not going your way today," she told him.

She felt reproached by his look of disappointment, but it did not make her relent as she drove home another way. She felt that she was being mean, but she felt that it was best. After this she saw little of him except in the presence of Faith.

113

Then something happened that brought them together and changed the course of both their lives.

Faith had a bad hemorrhage, the terror of all tuberculosis sufferers, the sword of Damocles which hung over everyone who had a lung cavity. Sometimes these hemorrhages were slight and caused no immediate danger, but sometimes they were severe when a larger vessel had given way beneath the onslaught of that deadly invasion of disease. Faith's was severe and for a time it seemed that she would die before it was checked. She was transferred to the dangerously ill ward which every patient dreaded, for they knew how hopeless their case must be when they were taken there.

When James arrived, he found her looking so near death that his heart almost stopped beating. Linda was sitting by the bed talking to her and though Faith could not speak, for she was too weak, a faint smile flitted across her face as she nodded weakly in response to Linda's words.

He sat on the other side and took her hand, so thin and lifeless, and held it tenderly. He couldn't speak for a moment, for he was so shocked and heartbroken that he was afraid he would break down if he uttered a word.

Faith turned to Linda and her voiceless lips formed the words she couldn't speak, "Tell him," they said.

"She wants you to know that she is not afraid," Linda told him. "I talked to her yesterday after you left. She had a slight hemorrhage, but it was checked soon and I stayed with her. She was so sure that she was in God's hands that she had no fear. She knew that whether she lived or died, it would be in God's plan for her and she was satisfied."

"But I'm not satisfied!" he cried desperately. "Can't they give her blood or something to get her well? They can't let her die! They can't! I need her so!"

"They're doing all that can be done," she assured him. "We'll have to leave her in God's hands and pray that He will take care of her."

Faith gave his hands a weak pressure and nodded while she smiled. Her lips formed the words, "I love you."

"I love you, darling," he said as he leaned nearer, "and

I'm not going to let you die. I need you here with me."

Just then the nurse came in with the doctor. James asked if he might stay with her, but he was advised to leave. She was to be given a sedative and would need absolute quiet. He left reluctantly, knowing that he could do nothing if he stayed and Linda promised to come back later and sit with her.

Faith rallied enough to talk to him when he came back the next day. Linda phoned him at the office to tell him that he need not come back that evening, for Faith was still sleeping and needed the rest.

The next day Faith greeted him with a smile and seemed so much stronger that he was encouraged.

"I'm glad that I can talk to you, Jimmie darling," she said in a weak, thin voice. "I did want to tell you not to worry about me. If it is God's will for me to live, I shall be glad, but if it is His will to take me home, I shall still be glad. I shall be with my mother and I know how happy she will be to see me safe with my Lord after all these years of refusing to listen to His voice."

"What about me?" he asked in stricken tone. "I won't have anyone. I shall be alone and I don't think I can stand it. You can't go and leave me, darling. I won't want to live without you."

"Linda will help you," she told him. "You will learn to love her as much as I do. She can take my place in your life and keep you from being lonely."

Her words startled him for a moment, then he realized that she had not meant what he had thought. The love she was talking about was that of friend for friend. He shook his head.

"No one can ever take your place."

Linda was standing in the doorway and had heard what they said. She turned to leave, hoping that they had not seen her. Faith's words had stirred up emotions which she had thought she had conquered. Faith saw her and beckoned to her to come in. She came to the bed and gave James a nod, then smiled down at Faith.

"I just dropped in to see how you are," she said. "I will

come back later and I'll stay with you as long as they will let me.''

"Please don't go," James begged. "You've been wonderful to her and she seems to gain strength by just having you near her. I shall have to leave soon."

"I'll be down the hall with Jane," she said. "I'll come back when you leave. Faith needs you."

She left them and walked slowly down the hall to the ward at the other end. She needed time to still the wild, rebellious beating of her heart. She did not feel like talking to anyone just now, but Jane needed her and she had promised to come. She had seen the look of surprise on James' face when Faith had spoken about her. She wondered what he thought. She felt like a thief as her heart kept up its mad pounding. She felt guilty that she should care for him, as guilty as if she had deliberately tried to take him away from Faith to whom he belonged. She knew that she could not control her rebellious heart and that she had never consciously given him anything but friendship and the effort to witness to him, with the hope that he would be saved, but she felt depressed and miserable while she tried to give a message from the Bible to Jane.

The next day she was with Faith when he came. Faith had had another hemorrhage and Linda had phoned for James to come at once. When he saw her ghastly face and the deep circles under her eyes, he knew that she was dying. She was barely conscious, but when he knelt by the bed and took her hand in his, her thin little hand which was already cold and almost lifeless, a glimmer of recognition crept into her eyes. Her bloodless lips curved in a faint smile, then in a few moments, like the flickering glimmer of a little candle flame, her life went out and her soul was on its way to join the mother who had prayed for her through the years and to meet the Lord who had been so longsuffering and so willing to receive her unto Himself.

James bowed his head upon the bed and sobbed convulsively, unashamed, like a child whose heart has been broken. Linda sat with tears in her own eyes. She had loved the small

116

sufferer as if she had been a child, though Faith was almost as old as she was. Faith was her child in the Lord. In her heart she was rejoicing that she had been permitted to lead this girl to Him and she bowed her head and offered a prayer of thanksgiving. Then she prayed earnestly that the heartbroken man on the other side of the bed might find peace in the only Source of peace and comfort.

An orderly came in presently with the roller that was to take Faith's body to the basement in the main hospital to await whatever arrangements were to be made. James was spared the sickening sight of that roller going down the hall with that small body wrapped in brown paper, a sight which brought a shudder of terror to every patient who saw it. He left with Linda and they went to the lobby in the main hospital. He knew nothing about funeral arrangements there and he asked her to advise him. Customs were often different in this city with its old-world atmosphere.

That night they sat alone in the funeral parlor. A few who worked with James at the office came to offer their sympathy and then left soon afterwards. A large spray from the office force lay upon the casket.

James rose and went again to look down at the lovely face so calm and peaceful in death. The pale gold hair framed her face with soft curls amd made that face appear more angelic than any artist could have painted it.

"She looks like a beautiful doll," he said in broken tones as Linda came and stood beside him. "She was such a helpless little thing, so dependent. When I was first forced to help her, I resented being bothered, but I grew to love it. Now there is no one. There's no use to go on living. There's nothing to go on for."

He turned away while tears coursed down his face unnoticed, and sat down while she came and sat beside him.

"You have much to live for," she told him. "You have your life before you and can make your life count for something, if you'll only try."

"What's the use?" he asked bitterly. 'Everything and everyone I've ever loved have been taken from me. There's

117

nothing left in my heart but hate. I hate the whole rotten lot of them who were responsible for her death. If she hadn't been sent to prison, she would have been alive now."

"Perhaps she would have lived a while longer, but she would have died before long. She had that cavity long before she went to prison," Linda told him, trying to take away some of the bitterness. "Please try to believe that she is far happier now than she could ever have been if she had lived. She told me not long ago that she was glad that this had happened to her. She said that if she had not come here, she would never, perhaps, have accepted Christ as her Saviour. She said she would be glad that this happened, even if she should die and never know the joy of being your wife."

"She said that?" he asked with wide, tear-filled eyes.

Linda nodded. "You see, the Lord meant more to her than even you. That is as it should be. It didn't mean that she loved you less, but that she had come to love Him more. But the love she had for the Lord was not the same as the love she had for you. It was something more precious."

"Well, I don't love Him!" he cried harshly. "He took her away from me when He knew that she was all I had left. He took everything else away and now her."

"He did it for a purpose. And His plan and purpose are always right. Perhaps someday you will realize and believe that He may have done it for your own soul's salvation."

He stared at her somberly. "I never could believe that. I don't want to believe it. I don't care a rap about my soul's salvation. All I'd like to do is to live long enough to make some people pay for what they have done to me."

She tried to keep him from seeing how shocked she was at his words and how they hurt her.

"Don't you ever want to see Faith again?" she asked.

"Of course I would want to, if I believed that I could, but I don't believe that there is anything after this life. I just can't believe it."

"Then you think that the change in her and what I have in my heart is all just a belief in some myth, that there is nothing to account for the miracle which you yourself acknowledged had changed Faith and transformed her despair to joy and hope? Do you believe that she went out of this life so peacefully and so joyfully just because she believed in something that did not exist?''

He shook his head without replying.

"I've seen many here who died without faith in God and I've seen others who had that faith and who died just as she died. I know that it was a belief in the truth that there is a life beyond this one, and that when her spirit left her body she knew that she would be with the Lord. If I didn't have that assurance, believe me, I wouldn't be down here trying to give these patients the same hope that she had. It's backbreaking, trying work, but it is worth everything to see someone experience the miracle that came to Faith. I know it is real and I urge you to believe that it is. You would have comfort in the trying days ahead and you would have something to live for and a hope to look forward to. You would have the love of God in your heart and He would help you bear your grief.''

"How could I ever have the love of God in my heart when there is nothing but hate there?'' he asked in heavy tones of misery. "I feel that I hate the whole world and that I even hate God.''

"If you would yield your heart and your will to Him and accept Jesus as your Saviour, God would wipe out that hate and give you love instead. And only love can carry you through dark days and trying times.''

He turned to her desperately and her heart was torn by the look of utter hopelessness in his eyes.

"I wish I could say that I could do this. I wish I had what you have, but you just don't know what is in my heart.''

"No, but God knows and He is willing to take out of your heart everything that should not be there. When His Spirit comes in, then everything else has to go but that which is pleasing to Him.''

He shook his head again in silence and went over once more to the casket where he stood looking down at the cold angelic face with eyes that were closed, eyes that could no longer respond to his with an adoring look, lips that could no longer respond to his kiss. Dry sobs shook him as he stood there. Linda sat for a moment wishing with all her heart that she had it in her power to comfort him, but she knew that she could do nothing more than she had tried to do. The rest was in God's hands. It was getting late and she arose to go.

"I hate to leave you here alone," she said, coming and standing beside him, "but it is getting late and I shall have to go. Mother will be worried. You had better go and get some rest. They will be closing soon. I shall be here tomorrow."

He turned to her appealingly.

"Don't leave me!" It was the cry of a helpless child. "I need you. Even if I can't do what you want me to do, I need you. You were a help to Faith and she said that you would help me. Please do! I shall be so alone."

"I'll be back tomorrow, but I must go," she said. "I'll drive you home if you'll let me."

"Thanks, but I'll get a cab later. Forgive me for being such a baby and being so selfish."

He took her hand and held it tightly between both of his.

"I can never forget what you did for her." His voice broke and for a moment he couldn't go on. "I shall always value your friendship, so please don't desert me. Let me see you once in a while. Please!"

"I will," she promised, then she left him.

As she drove home there were tears coursing down her cheeks, but they were not tears of grief for him or for Faith. They were tears for her own aching heart, her rebellious heart which would not obey her will to kill a love that should not be there.

She must drive it out of her heart, for it was not right for her to let it remain there, but she did not want to drive it out. She prayed silently for strength to be the victor in this, the greatest struggle she had ever had. She knew, even as she prayed, that if she were victor, there would also be sorrow and longing in that vacant place where love had been. But God was able and she knew that He would give her strength to do what she should.

CHAPTER 16

THE FUNERAL SERVICE was short and simple. James had left everything to Linda, for, now that Faith was gone, nothing mattered. There were only a few there, three or four from the office and Mrs. Thomas, but he was scarcely aware of the presence of anyone.

True to her promise, Linda came early. He greeted her with a nod and a solemn face. Her heart ached with sympathy for him. His face was haggard and he showed the effects of the strain and grief of the past few days.

Linda had asked her pastor to take charge of the service and he said a few words that should have been a comfort to James, but he did not even hear them. His mind was on the past, that other funeral service where he had been the only mourner when his mother had been laid away. He was thinking of the day he had first met Faith, her bewildered helplessness when she had arrived in the city and her aunt had not been there to meet her. He remembered how irritated he had been because he felt that he had to help her and how anxious he had been to be rid of her and how impatient he had been when the days dragged by and he still had her problems on his hands.

If he only had her back and could live those days over

again, how differently he would act. How precious she had become and what a joy it had been to look after her and to feel her dependence upon him. In just a few minutes he would look upon her face for the last time and he would face an empty world utterly alone.

His tortured eyes wandered to Linda sitting nearby and their gaze met. There was such sympathy in her eyes that he felt his heart melt and the sting of tears in his eyes. He was not alone. He still had her. He could rely upon her sympathy and her strength to help him through the dark days ahead. He sighed as he turned away. He didn't want her to see the tears. It seemed weak to have tears in the presence of these people who were sitting solemnly, trying to feel a sympathy that they could not feel. None could bear or share the pain of another heart, no matter how much they might try. Each must, after all, bear his own pain and bear it alone. The sympathy which friends might express would help, in a sense, for it did help to know that friends cared how one suffered, but they could not enter into the pain of a single heartache. There was only One who could do that and James did not know that One.

The One who had suffered and died and shed His blood knew and understood every heartache that man could experience had offered to share that suffering and help man to bear it. But James had refused to turn to Him who could have softened the blow and lessened the grief, who could have shared it and given comfort and peace to his broken heart.

As the minister finished his final prayer James arose and went to take a last look at the still, lovely face before it was taken from him forever. The memory of it would always be engraved upon his heart. He turned away and went blindly to the waiting car. He had asked Linda if she would ride with him, for there was no one else except the minister going to the cemetery.

They drove to the plot where the short service was finished and then the ugly pit that received the small body was covered with a blanket of artificial grass and the few flowers that had been on the casket.

On the way home they rode for a time in silence. James sat with bowed head and body slumped dejectedly in a corner of the car. Linda's heart ached as she looked at him. She had never known sorrow such as this, but she felt that she knew how much he must be suffering. He was utterly alone. She could not bear to sit silently by without trying to say something that would help him.

"Words are inadequate," she said, "but I want you to know that I sympathize with you as much as anyone can with another at a time like this. I wish I could help you bear your grief, but that is impossible. Only God can do that."

She had not meant to mention God, for she knew how bitter he was and how absolutely devoid of belief or the desire to believe, but it had slipped out involuntarily. She was so used to talking about Christ to everyone who gave her the opportunity, that the words were always on the tip of her tongue.

He raised his head and turned his dull eyes to meet hers.

"How could you expect me to believe that God could help me when He took her away from me?"

"I'm sorry. I didn't mean to annoy you by saying that. The words came without my realizing it. I suppose it was because I'm so used to telling those who need Him what a comfort He can be. It's because I turn to Him with every heartache and every problem that comes to me and I have found Him to be a help and a comfort."

"You've never had anything to hit you as deep as this," he said.

"No, I haven't," she admitted, "but I know that God is just as able to meet the big problems and comfort the deep heartaches as He is to cope with those that are not so big. As we go through life we are bound to have heartaches and I don't mean to say that when we belong to the Lord we will never have any, but I do say that He promises to be near those who have broken hearts, because He understands and knows just how we feel. That is why I was anxious for you to know Him and to belong to Him before this happened, because I knew how much you would need Him."

He turned away and looked out of the window.

"All I need is to forget. If I were a drinking man I'd go out and get so drunk that I wouldn't be able to think for days."

"What good would that do? You can't erase memory by getting drunk. You'd only weaken your strength and befuddle your mind so that you wouldn't be able to do your work, but it wouldn't wipe out memory. I don't think you want to forget Faith. Her memory will always be with you, no matter how long you may live. I shall never forget her either, for I learned to love her. The only difference between your memory and mine is that I know she is far happier now with the Lord and her loved ones than she could ever have been here and I know that I shall see her again. Since you don't believe what she so gladly accepted as the truth, for you there is no hope for the future. How I wish that I could impart that hope and comfort to you!"

"How I wish you could!" he exclaimed.

"I would gladly, if I could, but only God can do that and you are not willing to give Him the chance."

"No," he replied with a sudden new note in his voice, a note of grim determination. "I've got a job to do and God has no place in it."

His voice was harsh and a look that she had never seen upon his face before crossed it like a dark shadow. She felt instinctively that it was something evil, something that perhaps had been holding him back all this time when the Spirit of God must have been speaking to him. She shrank from the thought, for the love she had fought against could have no part in a thing like this. She could not refrain from making one more desperate effort to turn his heart to God.

"If there is no place for God in this thing that you have set yourself to do, I beg of you to forget it. No matter what it is, if it is something that God would not approve of, it will only bring you more sorrow in the end and take you farther away from God. Please don't think of it. Give it up, I beg of you."

He shook his head stubbornly.

"It's been my plan for too long. It's become a part of my life. It brought me here to the city. I had to let it drop while Faith was here. Now that she is gone, I shall get the job done or keep trying as long as I live."

"I shall pray that God will hinder you," she said slowly as her solemn eyes met his. "I shall pray that He will not let you do anything that might hinder you from receiving the salvation that you so sorely need, for without it you are lost."

He stared at her a moment in silence, then said, "Please don't pray for me. I'm not worth it."

"Faith thought you were," she reminded him. "And I think you are."

"She loved me and couldn't see anything but good in me."

His words brought a quicker beating to her heart and she answered quickly, so that he might not see what she felt and what she feared might be revealed in her eyes as they met his. Her love cried out within her, even though she felt guilty because she loved him when he was not even interested in the Lord or in his salvation.

"God loves you even though He sees the bad as well as the good in you. He knows just what that thing is that you say you have to do and He knows just what harm it might bring into your life if you are able to accomplish it. That is why I shall pray that He will hinder you from doing it."

"That will not stop me," he declared.

They were approaching the place where he was to get out. She had left her car at the funeral home and would pick it up there. He turned to her appealingly.

"May I see you again soon?"

"I don't know how soon that can be. I am kept pretty busy."

She thought that it would be best if she did not see him again. She had done everything she could and to no avail, to win him for the Lord. If she did not see him again, this love which she felt she had no right to keep in her heart would be forgotten more quickly.

"Is it because I don't believe as you do, because I've

125

been so stubborn in refusing to believe?'' he asked desperately.

"Perhaps. If I can't be of help to you there is no point in my seeing you again. We have nothing in common."

"We have the love for Faith," he argued. "She said you would help me in my loneliness. Please don't give me up as a hopeless case. I do need you and who knows, if you let me see you occasionally, I might even one day believe as you do."

She smiled in spite of her heavy heart.

"I wish I could believe that you are sincere in what you've just said, but I'm afraid that it's just an excuse and a flimsy one."

"It isn't," he said seriously. "I need you. I'll be lost and lonely. Whenever I'm with you I seem to have more peace in my heart than at any other time, even though what you say sometimes upsets me. I won't ask much. Just let me talk to you sometimes when I feel as if I can't go on. That little will help so much."

"I can't refuse to talk to you," she told him as the car stopped.

"Then may I phone you sometime?"

"Of course you may."

As she rode away she wondered what it was that he had on his mind, this thing that he must do, the thing which she felt was keeping him from the Lord. She was determined to pray that God would hinder him from doing whatever it was, for she knew that it would only wreck his soul. She was not thinking of her love for him just now. She was thinking of his soul, of the yearning that Faith had for that soul, that it might be redeemed as hers had been. She would pray, for she knew that her Lord was able to do exceeding abundantly above all that she asked.

CHAPTER 17

FOR THE THIRD TIME James had the task of disposing of the possessions of someone who had gone out of life. It had seemed such a short time since he had had to dispose of his mother's clothes and furniture, and since he had helped Faith as she went through her aunt's possessions. Now he would have to do the same with hers. Mrs. Thomas, of course, wanted to get them out of the way as soon as possible. She had stored everything, for Faith's room had been rented when she went to the hospital.

There were only her clothes and luggage and a few little keepsakes, some photos of her mother and father and of herself. He tore up the pictures of her parents, for he knew that she would want that, but he kept the pictures of herself. She had not changed much since the last one was taken and he felt the tears sting his eyes as he looked at it. She was smiling from the picture as he had seen her smile so often when he told her that he loved her.

Mrs. Thomas was there helping him and she looked at him with sympathy in her eyes. She knew how he must be suffering, for she had passed through her own time of loss and pain.

With a sigh he put the pictures in his pocket and turned

to Mrs. Thomas. "You take her clothes and do with them what you think best," he said. "I don't know what to do with them."

"I'll find someone who needs them," she told him and she put them back into the suitcase.

He went back to his room and sat with his head bowed upon his hands. He had never felt so lost even when his mother had died. He returned to work the next day with a heavy heart and a gloomy outlook on life. There was no incentive to go on. When he returned to his room after a lonely dinner, he got out his list of names and the city map and began to look them over. He had not yet finished his mission. Now there was nothing to hinder him from going ahead with his search for Thomas Martin.

He sat up late looking over the list of names and studying his map. He wanted to get so tired that he would not lie awake thinking, for thinking meant suffering.

The next day at noon he began his search once more. It proved to be a failure. The man who bore the name of Martin did not resemble the picture in the least and he was a much younger man than his intended victim would be.

The telephone book seemed to be as full of Martins as it was of Smiths and Joneses and it stretched out before him, making him weary just to look at it. He went through the list day after day at his lunch hour and in the evening, wearing himself out and all to no purpose, for not one of those whom he contacted was the man he sought. His better judgment told him to give up, that it was foolish for him to keep on searching. It was worse than the proverbial needle in the haystack, but he would not give up; not, he vowed, until he had seen the last man on that list and had to admit that he had failed.

The hatred that had seethed within him grew as the days passed until he became morose and withdrew into himself so that he was not even friendly with those in the office who had shown him kindness. They decided to ignore him and he was more lonely than ever. Whenever he thought of Faith, it only added fuel to the flame of his anger and rebellion at the injustice which had condemned his father to death in prison. And Faith's death was unnecessary. If it had not been for the law's stupid blunder, she might not have died.

To be tricked and bludgeoned by fate this second time was just too much. There was no justice anywhere. And God couldn't be a God of love if He allowed such things to happen to innocent people. James was lost in a world of darkness created by his own bitterness and hatred which he nursed until it became a monster which threatened to destroy his soul.

He did not phone Linda even though sometimes he longed to see her and have contact with her quiet peace and her gentleness combined with strength. He felt the need of her, but she had made him feel that she was no longer interested in him. She had most surely thrown up a barrier to his hopes to see her. He knew that her plea of being busy was just an excuse. She may have been busy, but he knew that she was no busier than she had been when she spent so much time with Faith. But he knew that she spent that time because it brought results. She knew that he was a hopeless case, so perhaps she did not want to waste any more time with him.

This only added to his bitterness and desperate loneliness. It was just one more proof that no one cared what became of him, no one wanted his friendship. Life was just an empty shell, with only heartaches and the desire for revenge as his companions.

If he had known why Linda had seemed so indifferent he would have been astonished, and life would have taken on a new meaning. He did not know how she longed to see him while she was trying valiantly to forget him and not yield to the cry of her heart for just a few moments with him. She tried to keep so busy that she would have no time to think of him, but her rebellious thoughts wandered persistently to him.

Wherever she went, the vision of his dark, handsome face with the grief-stricken eyes would appear before her. The echo of his voice pleading for just a few moments of her time would awaken a longing in her heart that she knew she could not overcome by the mere will to do so. She found herself waiting anxiously for the phone call which never came, then as the days passed she became nervous and worried for fear something had happened to him. She tried to pray about this love which she felt was wrong, but her prayers seemed to come just from her lips and not from her heart.

She shared her mother's anxiety about her father. He had been growing slowly worse through the months. He had been on the downgrade physically for some time, but neither they nor the doctor had thought it anything serious. It had started with stomach ulcers which had caused only a mild discomfort and had been benefited by treatment, but there seemed to be some obscure trouble which was sapping his strength, but which the physician could not diagnose.

He seldom left his room now, but sat day after day, when he was not in bed, with head sunk upon his breast, refusing to be cheered by any effort that Linda and her mother made to draw him out of his gloom and despondency.

Linda grieved because he was not a Christian. She and her mother had done their utmost to make him see the need of salvation, but he had turned a deaf ear to their efforts and finally he had forbidden them to talk about it any more. They had prayed that in some way God would open his hardened heart and let him see the light before it was too late, but it seemed to Linda as she grieved over him that her prayers were not being answered and she began to fear that they never would be. But she still had faith for she knew that God knew the end from the beginning, so she continued to pray and to hope and she tried to be cheerful for her mother's sake.

One evening when she was sitting in her room reading and trying to concentrate on what she read instead of thinking about James, the phone rang and she heard his voice on the other end of the line. She could scarcely keep the joy out of her voice as she answered, but she managed a calm reply.

"I hate to bother you when you're so busy," he said, "but I'm so lonely that I can't stand it any longer. Do you mind if I talk to you for a little while?"

"Why, no," she said, trying to keep her voice steady. "Not at all. I'm not that busy. I'm really sorry I told you that."

If he only knew how sorry she was, he would drop the phone and come to her home immediately. Then he might see the joy that would be shining in her eyes at the sight of him. But she had no right to a joy like that. His love belonged to Faith. She still held it in her little hands, even though those little hands were cold in death.

"I figured you didn't want to be bothered with my troubles any longer." His voice sounded from the depths of woe. "I've been a nuisance to you."

"But you haven't," she insisted. "I was glad to be of what little help and comfort I could be when I felt that you needed me. When you didn't call, I thought that you no longer needed me."

How illogical could she be, she wondered, and how stupid those words were! What would he think of her?

"I didn't call because I thought from what you said that you really didn't want me to call."

She laughed, a happy little laugh that somehow brought a thrill to his heart and made him feel suddenly less downcast.

"This conversation isn't getting anywhere, it is?" she remarked. "Did you want to talk to me about something in particular or did you just want to while away a lonely hour?"

"I would love to be able to see you if you would let me," he told her, "but if you're too busy for that, I just wanted to hear the sound of your voice. It's been so long since I've talked to anyone who even wanted to be friends. Could I see you sometime?"

She hesitated a moment while she fought a losing battle between desire and better judgment, then she said, "Of course you may if you want to. If you want to come, I shall be glad to talk to you."

It sounded stiff and priggish, but she was trying to restrain her eagerness from showing in her words or her voice.

"How good you are to let me worry you with my troubles again! May I come to see you tomorrow evening?"

"Yes, you may. Do you know how to find my house?"

He said he thought he did. He had studied the map enough to enable him to get almost anywhere. She gave him directions, however, and he hung up feeling more light-hearted than he had since Faith had left him.

CHAPTER **18**

LINDA SEEMED EVEN MORE LOVELY than James had remembered her when she met him at the door. She had on a simple dress of navy with a white collar that suited her dark beauty to perfection. He had never seen her in anything but the white uniform she wore when she was at the hospital, except at the funeral home and he wasn't even aware then of what she wore. He had been lost in his sorrow.

Her smile brought a quicker beating to his heart and his lips answered her smile and the light in her eyes.

"It's good to see you again after all these ages," he said as she led the way into the living room. "You can't imagine how I've missed you and how I've longed to have the opportunity to see you again."

"I'm sorry that I made you feel that I didn't want to see you again," she apologized as they sat down together on the couch. "But let's forget it. I've been wondering how you were getting along. I know how lonely you must be and I do want to help you if I can."

"You can help me by just letting me come to see you when you have time to talk to me. I've tried to pass away the lonely hours after dinner until bed time but it's been terrible. Nothing seems to hold my interest. What joy can you have in life? What do you do to have a good time?" he asked.

She spoke slowly, choosing her words carefully. It was sheer joy to him to watch her. He had forgotten Faith completely for the moment and, for the first time since her death, he was not burdened with his sorrow. While Linda talked, he admired her beauty which was enhanced by the color that rose in her clear skin and the mellow light in her dark eyes when she talked about her belief in God. "I have a wonderful time trying to serve the Lord. Since I gave up many things when I became a Christian, the Lord has supplied me with other things that are much better and which give me much more lasting happiness. I teach a Sunday school class and it takes time to prepare the lessons. While I'm studying my Bible, I see things in it that I never saw before and I get a blessing from what I find. That gives me joy, much joy."

He shook his head and remarked, "I can't see any joy in that."

"That's because you don't have the love of God in your heart. If you did, you would love His Word and every time you found something new in it, you would feel that you had made a wonderful discovery."

"Don't you ever look at television?" he asked.

"Sometimes, when I have time," she answered with a smile. "Then there is my hospital work. It has brought me my greatest joy, for there is nothing more wonderful to a Christian than to lead someone to Christ. That takes up a great deal of my time and I often come home worn out, but I wouldn't give it up for anything in the world. Too many on the brink of eternity have gone out to be with the Lord because He gave me the privilege of leading them to Him before it was too late."

Mention of the hospital brought back memory of Faith. She saw the pain in his eyes and she understood.

"I know what you're thinking," she said in tones of sympathy, "but just think of how happy your little Faith was because she found the peace and joy in her heart that came when she found the Lord."

"It's all too deep for me," he said.

The light had vanished from his eyes and the joy from his heart. He was once more plunged in gloom.

"I also have my music," she said, trying to help him to be cheerful again. "I love to play the piano. I don't play too well, but I enjoy it. I sing in the choir and that takes up some of my time. Many of the young people in the choir are my close friends and we enjoy being together at choir practice as well as at other times. So you see, my life is full and I'm quite happy, far more so than I was when I was living my own life and not in the center of the will of the Lord."

"I've always loved music. Would you play something for me?" he asked.

"I'd be glad to." She got up and closed the door leading upstairs. "Dad might be resting and I don't want to disturb him," she explained. "He hasn't been at all well and Mother and I are concerned about him."

He expressed his sympathy as she went to the piano and began to play a number that seemed difficult to him. While she played he had a chance to look about the room. It was attractively, though not lavishly, furnished. There was nothing stiffly ornamental in the furnishings, but the room gave the impression that it was meant to be lived in and enjoyed. The house itself was large enough to speak of comfort and moderate wealth. It was in one of the newer sections of the city near the lake front. He wondered as he listened to her playing and watched the rapid flitting of her slender fingers over the keyboard, what business Mr. Martinez was engaged in.

As she continued to play he sat watching her face. She seemed absorbed in what she was playing, for she did not look at him, but, with head slightly raised, she seemed to be looking at something in the far distance, something which his eyes could not behold. He did not know what she was playing, but the number was her own variation of "I Love to Tell the Story." There was a rapt look on her face and he realized that, for the moment, she was unaware of him. Her thoughts were in some faraway place. He wished that he might go with her to that place where her thoughts were leading her, for there was a new light upon her face and a brighter glow in her eyes.

She stopped suddenly and turned to catch his absorbed, admiring gaze fixed upon her and her heart began a wild beating. She had never seen that look in his eyes before. It was more than a warm friendly gleam. It was something that wakened a faint hope in her heart, but which brought the disturbing knowledge that she should not rejoice over it. This man was not a Christian and she must not let her love for him grow. But how could she prevent it when she met that look in his eyes? She gave him a smile.

"You did a dangerous thing when you asked me to play. When I sit at the piano and begin playing those beautiful old hymns, I usually forget everything else and I'm liable to go on and on unless someone stops me."

"I don't want to stop you. I wish you would go on," he said eagerly. "What is the name of that piece? It is beautiful."

"It's just my own version of an old favorite, 'I Love to Tell the Story.' I often find myself humming it when I'm working about the house. I sang it once as a solo when I was just a tiny girl."

"Please sing something for me," he urged.

"If you can sit through it. I warn you that I'm no Jenny Lind."

She sang another of her favorites, an old song, "The End of a Perfect Day." When she came to the beginning of the last verse, "When I come to the end of a perfect day and the end of a journey too," she closed her eyes and raised her face while her voice poured forth in muted melody that thrilled him and wakened something within him that startled him.

He had a sudden desire to take her in his arms and kiss her. This shocked him, for he felt that he was being disloyal to Faith's memory by harboring such a desire. He could not help it, however, for she was beautiful and desirable with that rapt look on her face. The very fact that it seemed to set her apart from him wakened a longing within him to bridge that separation and get closer to her secret thoughts, to be nearer to her heart.

She finished the song and turned to him with a smile but when she saw the look in his eyes, the smile vanished and she drew her breath in quickly with a surprised gasp.

"I think that's one of the most beautiful and touching songs I've ever heard, though it is so old," she said, trying to cover up her embarrassment over that startled gasp. She hoped that he did not notice it, for he might be embarrassed to know that she had discovered what he had not intended for her to see.

"It is beautiful," he replied, though he had scarcely heard the song. "Your voice is beautiful," he added truthfully, for he was aware of that, even in the disturbing confusion of his desires. "Please sing something else."

"Suppose you join me. I'm sure you can sing," she suggested.

"I haven't tried to sing for a long time. I sang a little when I was in high school, in choruses, but that doesn't mean I can sing."

"Let's try anyway."

He came and stood by her at the piano while she played the introduction to a simple melody that she was sure he must know. It was a song that was popular just then and he nodded when she asked him if he were familiar with it.

"This is the kind of song that Dad likes," she explained. "I used to sing it for him. Lately he has been so nervous and so ill that he doesn't even want to hear me play."

There was a touch of sadness in her voice, but she gave him a smile as she began to sing and nodded for him to join her.

"Why, you have a good voice," she told him when they had finished. She gave him a speculative look. "I could use that voice if you would be willing."

"Use my voice!" he echoed in surprise. "How?"

"We need more male voices in our young people's choir," she told him. "I would love to have you sing with us if you would."

"Oh! I don't think I could do that," he exclaimed. "I would love to do anything that would repay you even in a small way for all you have done for Faith and for me, but I'm afraid I couldn't sing in a church choir. I don't think they would want me, if they knew how I feel about spiritual matters."

That was not what he was thinking. What would they think of him if they knew what he was doing every day, that he was searching for a man in order to kill him? What would the congregation think if it ever became known that one of their choir members was a murderer? What would Linda think of him if she ever knew? The thought brought a spasm of pain. She would turn from him in horror. He had had that same fear about Faith when she was living. But she had told him that it didn't matter what he was or what he had done. It would be different with Linda. And, he suddenly realized, it would have been different with Faith after she had had this change which Linda called conversion. She also would have turned from him in horror. He felt like an outcast and suddenly the joy he had had in his heart all evening forsook him.

Linda was looking at him with serious eyes.

"Those young people know what it is to serve the Lord," she informed him gravely, "and they know what it is to have compassion and understanding for one who has not yet found that joy. I think they would be glad to have you join them. They might help you to bear your loneliness and you would surely be helping us by using your voice. Think it over."

She was thinking that this might be another opportunity to win him for the Lord.

He saw that it was getting late and he felt that he should be going. He wanted to go, yet he hated to leave her. He seemed to have entered a different world since he had been in her presence and he hated to leave it and go back into his own dark world of hate and the plan for murder.

"May I see you again soon?" he asked when he finally said that he must be going. "It's been heavenly being here with you and it was good of you to let me come."

"Call me when you feel too lonesome," she said. "I'll be glad to have you come, if I have no other engagement. In the meantime think about the choir. You would be helping me a lot if you would consent to join us."

He promised to think about it, but he felt that he could never do what she asked. On his way home, however, his determination not to grant her request weakened. It would give him the opportunity to be with her much more often than he could hope for otherwise. That thought outweighed his conviction that he had no right to join the choir.

When he reached his room and tried to sleep, the conflict between desire and better judgment battled within him for a long time before sleep and oblivion finally came.

CHAPTER 19

JAMES WANTED TO CALL LINDA the next day and ask if he might come again, but he restrained his desire. He didn't want to annoy her. He knew that she had other friends and other engagements and might not have an evening free for some time. Perhaps she had given him this one evening because he had begged for it.

He continued his search for Thomas Martin with stubborn persistence, but underneath the hate he had kept alive in his heart and his determined effort to find his man, there was a subtle feeling of relief each time he met with failure.

He called at offices and at the homes of all the Martins on his telephone list and then he turned to the city directory to see if he might find his victim there. He did not want to let one name pass without being investigated. He was beginning to think that his man was either dead or that he had left the city. In either case his search would be ended and his purpose in life would meet with defeat.

As time passed and the memory of his visit with Linda remained with him and the urge to see her again was ever present with him, he felt that if he failed a great load would be lifted from him. He began to believe, in the light of what she had said so often, that he would never have peace if he did commit the murder he contemplated and he longed for the peace and calm which she so beautifully manifested.

But, he argued, would he ever know what that peace meant, would he ever be able to possess that peace even if he did not commit that murder? How could he, when he didn't seem to be able to believe what she believed, what Faith had believed so easily and so completely? But then, Faith had had the teaching of her mother. That made it easy for her to receive what she already believed. He wondered what had led Linda to accept her belief in Christ as her Saviour. He wondered what her mother and father were like, whether they were Christians like herself. He thought he would ask her when he saw her again. He had no idea when that would be, for he knew that if he went to see her again, she would want to know what he had decided about joining the choir. He had not made up his mind what he should do.

As time passed and his loneliness again bore down upon him, he couldn't stand it any longer, so he phoned her and asked when he might see her again.

"Could I come tonight?" he asked. "It's been a long time and the time has dragged since I was there. I don't want to annoy you, but I would surely love to come if you have no other engagement."

"I'm sorry, but I have another engagement tonight," she replied.

The sound of her low melodious voice thrilled him and he realized how much her friendship meant to him.

"Tonight is choir practice," she explained. "How about coming over and going with me and meeting the others? I'm sure you will like them. They are a wonderful group of young people and we all have a good time together."

He hesitated. He wanted to go just to be with her, but he felt that they might feel intuitively what he had in his heart and that they would shun him. The longer he persisted in his search, the more he felt that this diabolical hatred which grew within him would eventually show to those who knew him. Without knowing what the Word of God said about this, he recognized the truth that as a man thinketh in his heart, so is he.

Just as surely as the belief that Linda had in God and the love which she professed for Him manifested itself to others in her radiant, attractive personality, just so must the hate and vengeful spirit which he held in his heart finally manifest itself to those around him.

The thought was an arresting one and it filled him with a fear and uneasiness which he had never experienced before. If it shone forth from within his heart as a black shadow on his life, she might see it and would turn from him. He didn't want that to happen. He was in an agony of indecision, torn between longing and fear.

"Let me think it over for a while longer," he finally said. "I would like to meet your friends, but I'm still just a little afraid that I would not fit in with them. Would you let me see you again before time for the next choir practice? I'd like to talk to you about it."

"If I can help you in any way, I shall be glad to."

He thought that some of the warm friendliness had left her voice and it brought a chill to his spirits.

"You can!" he cried desperately. "You're the only one who can. When may I come?"

"I'll be free Monday evening. Will that suit you?"

"Any time will suit me," he declared. "I'll be there, and thank you for letting me come."

Sunday dragged by on leaden hours. He slept late to make the day shorter, then went out to a late breakfast. He went to the same little restaurant where he and Faith had had so many happy hours together. He had not been there since she died. He felt that he couldn't stand the memories that would haunt him there, but this morning, without thinking, he turned in that direction. He ordered his breakfast and watched the few customers idly while he waited for it. When he had almost finished eating, he suddenly realized where he was and the knowledge startled him. He had not once remembered that this was where he and Faith usually ate and he hadn't even thought of her the whole time. No haunting memories of her presence tormented him. He was glad and at the same time sad. He felt rebuked that he had forgotten her so soon. He felt that he had been disloyal to her memory. Yet he was glad that the keenness of his grief had faded. Time had done its work. He would never forget her completely, but she would remain as a dear sweet memory of days that were gone. That phase of his life has passed. He must live in the present. The future was something he did not care to contemplate.

He thought of Linda. She would be preparing to get ready for church by now. He felt that it would do him good to slip into her church and sit where he could not be seen, but where he could see her in the choir. Just the sight of her would cheer him. He could also get a chance to look over the others in the choir.

He hadn't been to church in so long that he could scarcely remember when he had been there last. He remembered that when he was a child he had been taken to Sunday school with his father and mother, though he had rebelled at being put in the class with a lot of other youngsters who were more inclined to argue and threaten a fist fight than they were to listen to a teacher struggle through a lesson which seemed senseless to his childish mind.

He remembered Linda saying that the church she attended was within walking distance of her home. When he returned to his room he got out his map and looked over the churches listed in the telephone book. He picked out the one which was nearest her home and decided to see if it were the right one. If not, he would leave and try the only other one nearby. If neither was the one, he would lose nothing and it would help to pass the time.

The first church he went to was not large, but was an attractive edifice. The congregation seemed to be just arriving for the service. He went in with them and took a seat in the last row. It would be easy for him to slip out if this were the wrong church.

He waited eagerly for the choir to come in. When they entered, wearing dark robes with white collars, he searched anxiously for Linda. Presently he saw her near the end of the line. She took her place in the middle of the front row. He did not notice what they were singing. He was conscious of nothing but the lovely girl singing with uplifted face, worshiping with her heart and soul as she sang.

The choir robe with the white collar made her look much younger than she really was. He could see that a number of the members were youngsters in their teens, but most of them were older, though Linda looked as young as any of them. None were as beautiful, he thought, as his eyes left her for a moment and traveled over the others.

When they sat down they were hidden from the congregation. Then the pastor began to read a passage from the Bible. He was a young man, perhaps thirty, and he had an attractive personality and a pleasant voice, but James was not interested in what he was reading. He wondered when the choir would sing.

After the prayer they rose to sing an anthem. He was delighted when Linda began to sing the solo part and he listened with rapt attention. Her voice was more lovely, he thought, than when he had heard her sing at her home. She had sung softly then. He supposed it was because she did not want to worry her father, but here it rang out strong and resonant, so that it seemed to fill the whole auditorium with its melody. The feeling that she put into the words touched his heart with a new emotion. He felt a sense of reverence for the One of whom she was singing. It was a version of that favorite of all psalms, "The Lord Is My Shepherd."

When she reached the last triumphant phrase of the song, "I shall dwell in the house of the Lord forever," her face became radiant with a rapt, joyous expression as she raised her eyes toward heaven and let the words ring out in a note of triumph. It seemed to him that a sigh rippled through the decorous congregation as the last note died while the organ played a soft interlude. James thought, as he watched her with his intense eyes that no heavenly being could look more angelic than she did, even though the robe she wore was somber black and not the white robe of angels he had seen in pictures.

When they had finished the anthem the pastor continued with the rest of the service, but James did not hear much that was said. He rose mechanically when the congregation rose and sat when they sat, but he was trying to understand what had taken place within him. This new sense of reverence for God puzzled him and he tried to analyze it. He had refused to believe in His love, for he had known nothing but hate most of his life. But he could not blame God for that hate. It had sprung from his own heart, a heart that did not acknowledge God in the plan of his life. Surely there must be a life after death, for Linda, with her knowledge and wisdom could not sing so rapturously about it if it were not a fact. He had closed his mind and heart to her words and to Faith's pleadings because he knew that he could not have the love of God in his heart and keep the hate which spurred him on. And he had stubbornly determined not to let that hate grow cold. Now, strangely, he wished that he could let it die. But he could not until he had followed every name on that list which was growing slowly smaller.

He was miserable as he sat with eyes fastened upon the minister, yet not hearing a word he said. He was like Sinbad the sailor, who had the old man of the sea upon his back and did not have the strength to release his powerful hold upon him. His own monster had grown in strength through the years until it had become the master of his life. He did not realize that it had been put there by the force of evil by which Satan sought to destroy his soul. He knew in that moment that he could never rid himself of it in his own power and yet he was not yet willing to call upon the One who alone was able to rid him of it.

He did not wait for the end of the service, but slipped out and walked for a long while upon the lake front, then sat down on the sea wall, trying to get order out of the chaos of his thoughts.

That night he felt impelled to go to the service once more. This time he listened to at least a part of the sermon and it left him more disturbed than ever. The preacher took for his text that familiar passage from Galatians, "Be not deceived, God is not mocked, for whatsoever a man soweth, that shall he also reap."

It was a simple message, containing nothing deep. It was an evangelistic message as were all of the minister's sermons at night. He explained so clearly how the results of sin brought forth evil fruit in the life, even though a person might receive forgiveness and salvation. One would not be judged for the sin he might have committed if he had received forgiveness for that sin, but most surely he would suffer the consequences of that sin. In all justice, God would allow one to suffer the consequences of that sin. He gave as an illustration the story of David, of how he had his faithful soldier, Uriah, murdered because David had wronged the man's wife and did not want to have his sin discovered. God forgave him when he repented with heartfelt sorrow, but God warned him that because he had had Uriah killed, the sword should not depart from his house. He pointed out that such might seem unjust, but that man cannot question God's dealings and God's laws are always just and perfect. Retribution came to David, with sorrow upon sorrow, but he was still God's man and God's promise to him was fulfilled when Jesus came to earth as a human being in the Davidic line, and who is now the only legal Heir to the throne of David which God had promised David centuries before Christ was born.

The sermon brought home to James more forcibly than ever his own predicament. It seemed that that sermon was directed toward him. He had murder in his heart and if he committed that murder, he would bear the fruit of that sin all the rest of his life, no matter what he might succeed in doing to hide it from man's law. God would surely know and even if he should ever accept Christ as his Saviour he would reap what he had sowed. He had never before considered the spiritual aspect of what he planned to do. He had been concerned only about his safety when he might be fleeing from the law. But now there stretched before him the thought of eternity. If his soul lived after this life and that murder was not forgiven, where would that soul be?

He had never believed in hell as an actual place but he shuddered nevertheless, at the thought, at the uncertainty of what eternity was. How sure Linda seemed! She knew what eternity held for her and, since that song she had sung in the morning service, he was inclined to think that she had grounds for her faith. Such faith could not be founded on hallucinations or mere hope. Faith had met death with that same sure knowledge. She knew where her soul was going and she had gone out into eternity with calm assurance.

On his way home James was still pondering over thoughts which left him disturbed and depressed. He was glad that he would see Linda the next evening. He looked to her to give peace and comfort to his disturbed mind, yet he knew that she could not impart peace. That would have to come from within, and for that to come something must go, hate and revenge. Could he let it go? No, not until he found that last man on his list and knew whether or not he had failed.

CHAPTER 20

THE MOMENT LINDA OPENED THE DOOR and greeted him with her engaging smile, James felt the warmth of her friendship and the glow of her beauty surround him. It entered his being in a strange new way and he felt a joy in her nearness such as he had never felt before. He had never felt this way even when he was with Faith.

This girl was different. She created the impression of strength and dependability, of staunchness and firmness and truth and life on a higher plane than he had ever known. Yet she was quiet and gentle and tender in her approach to a person. Faith had created nothing. He had loved her because she was beautiful and little and frail and helpless. With her he had felt strong and masterful, her guardian and protector. He felt that he would be happy just having her with him when he could bask in her love and in the joy of her nearness and even in her weakness.

With Linda it was different. She might look to the man she married for love and tenderness and happiness, but she would never be absolutely helpless or dependent upon anyone. There was a strength within her which came from some hidden source to which she could turn in any crisis. He began to realize that what she had tried to make him understand was true, that she did not depend upon her own strength but that she had learned to look to the only One who could impart strength of character and lift a person to the heights which no one could reach unless he sought that same Source.

"It's been ages," he remarked as she led the way to the living room, and they sat down together.

"Whose fault has it been?" she asked with raised eyebrows and a faint smile.

"I was afraid I would annoy you. I felt that you had just let me come before because I had begged. I was afraid that you really didn't want to be bothered with me any more. I'm a hopeless case."

"You're wrong," she replied seriously. "In the first place I wasn't being bothered by you. I was interested in you because I thought that you were lonely and sad and I wanted to help you. And as for you being a hopeless case, there are no hopeless cases with God. I was hoping that you would come again, but I couldn't ask you to come. That was up to you."

"That's not the way I've heard it," he said. "Most girls I've known keep the wire hot chasing some fellow they've met."

"I haven't learned the rules of the chase yet," she said as her smile appeared again. "I'm too busy to want to learn."

"I'm sure you never will," he told her. His eyes became serious and as they looked at her lovely face with a yearning look of which he was not aware, it brought the color to her face and a guilty pounding to her heart. "I like you just as you are."

"Thank you, sir." She bowed her head with an exaggerated motion of deference. "Tell me how you've been getting along," she said, hastening to change the subject.

"As usual. Nothing more exciting than the grind of work. It's strange, though, as the days pass so uneventfully and seemingly so slowly, it will soon be a year since Faith died. I can't believe it."

"Time has a way of slipping by. That is why I feel that it is important to put every hour to account and not to waste time idly when there is much to be done before the Lord comes or before He calls us home.''

"Don't you ever have a thought that doesn't include God?'' he asked. He couldn't understand this attitude. It puzzled him. "It must be a terrible strain to have to keep thinking of God all the time.''

She laughed, a clear rippling laugh that revealed her even, white teeth.

"It isn't a strain. I don't force myself to think of God. He's just a part of my life and thoughts of Him come as naturally as thoughts of Mother and Dad. When you love someone you are bound to think of him. And you want to do the things that will please him. I love my parents, so I want to do the things that please them, if I am an obedient child. Just the same way, since I belong to the Lord and love Him, I want to do the things that please Him. Trying to win souls is one way I know of that I can please Him. I feel that I do little for Him when He has done much for me. Feeling as I do, how can I do otherwise than have Him in my thoughts constantly? It's a joy, not a strain.''

He was silent. She leaned nearer and said softly, "Time has a way of softening the keenness of grief. I do hope that it has done that for you.''

"It has," he admitted, "but you have helped to make the grief more bearable.''

"I'm afraid I've had little opportunity to do that.''

"But you have. Just thinking of you has helped, even though I couldn't see you. You did something for me the very first time I ever saw you, even though I didn't realize it then. I'm sure you don't know when that was.''

"No, I don't, unless it was when I was talking to Faith that day we met.''

"No. It was one day when I saw you talking to Jane and reading to her from the Bible. It seemed to me then that you were different from anyone I'd ever seen. There was something in your face and in your eyes that intrigued me because I didn't know what it was. There was a light in your eyes and your face seemed to radiate an inner glow that made it so beautiful I couldn't keep from staring at you. I think you are very, very beautiful," he said suddenly, solemnly, as his eyes met hers.

She lowered hers a moment, unwilling to meet his earnest gaze. This was no idle compliment. She had received many of those and she paid little attention to them, but this was something different. She was afraid that he would discover some evidence of the joy that swept through her at his words. She could not let that happen.

"Thank you," she said soberly. "I appreciate that. I thank God for whatever beauty He may have given me, but what makes me more thankful and happy is when someone can see the beauty of Christ within me."

"I saw it that day." He spoke slowly, as if he had just been enlightened. "I didn't know what it was then, but I think I know now. The man who wins your love will have a treasure far beyond what any man could deserve."

She smiled. "He may realize that he has been cheated and that this treasure is not all he thought it was. I'm not perfect by any means."

"I think he would be willing to take the risk. Tell me," he asked suddenly, "is there someone?"

She gave him a startled glance and he hastened to apologize.

"I'm sorry. I shouldn't have asked that. It's none of my business. Please forgive me."

He was afraid that he had offended her and he did not want that to happen. The thought that she might be in love with someone gave him a moment of uneasiness. If she should marry, he would be denied the joy of her friendship. At least he could not have these moments alone with her and her friendship would mean little to him then. Something wonderful would be taken out of his life and where would he be then? He had no intimate friends, and aside from her there was no one else.

"You look as if you had suddenly lost your last friend," she said playfully. "I forgive you for asking such a personal question, so let's forget it."

"I was thinking how dreadful it would be if you should get married and I couldn't come to see you. I'd surely be miserable. I'd be alone."

"Don't worry about that until it happens," she advised.

She went to the piano and began to play softly so that he could not see her face. If he only knew what a sudden turmoil his question had stirred within her!

He came over presently and stood beside her and watched her while she played. She was able to meet his eyes with a gaze that was clear and friendly again, for she had been able to conquer her emotions and she was sure that no telltale light lingered in her eyes.

"How about joining me in a few numbers?" she suggested.

"I'll try, but you'll have to teach me. I don't know any of the songs you play."

She helped him and they sang several together, then she played a few others at his request. He had not intended to tell her that he had been to her church but he told her when she had finished.

"I was there at both services," he said.

"I'm glad you came!" she exclaimed. "How did you find the church?"

"You said it was near here so I selected one and got it right the first time."

"I hope you enjoyed the sermon. The one in the morning was especially helpful to Christians. The one at night was a real evangelistic message. Which one did you like more?"

"I didn't hear much of the one in the morning," he confessed. "I just sat there hoping that I'd hear you sing again. I did enjoy that solo part in the anthem that you sang. It was beautiful and your voice was lovely."

"That's one of my favorite anthems," she told him. "Did you hear the night sermon or were your thoughts wandering again?"

"I heard it, but I didn't care for it. It upset me too much. I was sorry that I had gone. Why do preachers preach such sermons? It seems to me that they ought to say things that bring peace to a person's heart instead of getting someone all stirred up.''

"The Word of God always does that when it strikes home to a heart that is not surrendered to Him,'' she said slowly. ''It brings peace only when there is nothing between a soul and the Lord. Otherwise it brings conviction or remorse of conscience or the knowledge that all is not right within. That is the Holy Spirit seeking that heart and pleading for entrance of the Word that will bring light and understanding and salvation.''

A sudden shadow settled on his face for he felt the truth of her words. The sermon had done just that for him, but he had stubbornly refused to listen to the pleading of the Spirit.

"What have you decided about joining the choir?'' she asked as he remained silent.

"I don't know. I've thought about it, but I haven't made up my mind.''

"Please decide that you'll join us. We really do need you and I'm sure that you will enjoy knowing the others. I ask it as a favor. I'd be glad if you would come. It would make me happy.''

"If you put it that way, I suppose I'll have to come,'' he said.

"Thank you.'' She gave him a radiant smile. ''We'll be looking for you.''

She felt that he was under conviction, though he might not realize it, if that sermon had disturbed him and she prayed earnestly after he had left that in some way it might lead to his salvation. She could not deny that her prayer was not entirely impersonal. This one soul was especially precious to her. There was no respect of persons with God, but there was with her. She was only human and he had become infinitely dear to her. If he were a Christian, nothing could prevent her from praying that one day perhaps he might love her and she would be free to give him her love.

The night seemed brighter and her sleep sweeter because of this hope, in spite of her father's condition and his hardened heart.

CHAPTER 21

JAMES PASSED THE INTERVENING DAYS until choir practice in a dither of uncertainty. He wanted to join the choir because Linda had said she wanted him and because it would give him the opportunity to be with her. He did want to meet more young people who might be congenial. It would help him in the loneliness which grew upon him as time passed. There was no one among his fellow employees with whom he could establish an intimate friendship. Most of the men were married or they were interested in sports which did not interest him. The few women who worked in his office were much older and not at all attractive.

He did not relish the idea of having to sit through two sermons each Sunday, if the sermon he had heard was a sample of what he would hear. It had been too distrubing. He wanted to banish disturbing thoughts instead of having them increased. He was being more disturbed as time passed by the voice of conscience which was raising a feeble protest against the task he had set for himself.

He had not been troubled by his conscience until he had fallen in love with Faith. Now that he had become better acquainted with Linda and could get a glimpse of the soul within her, his conscience bothered him constantly. If the preacher's sermons added to his unrest and this accusing voice within him became stronger, where would he be? He would be torn between two forces battling within him, the knowledge of the crime which he contemplated and the inevitable end if he carried out his plan, and the knowledge of failure if he gave up his plan and let the lust for vengeance die within him.

Since he had promised Linda that he would be at choir practice, he could not fail to go. He wanted to go by for Linda and go with her, but he thought that he had better not. She might have someone else who went with her. The thought was not pleasant. She was there when he entered the church and greeted him cordially, then introduced him to the others.

"We have a new baritone to help us," she remarked. "Isn't that good news?"

They agreed that it was and they greeted him with words that made him feel welcome.

"I'm afraid I won't be much help," he told them. "I can't read music very well and really I'm not much of a singer."

"That's why we have practice," laughed one of the boys. "I can't read music at all except to see when the notes go up or down. But you'll learn if you just stick to it as I'm doing. I'm sure you'll enjoy it just as much as we do. We may not have any great talent, but what little we have we want to use for the Lord."

James smiled a rather sickly smile. He hadn't expected a comment like this from a fellow, even though he had come to expect it from Linda. Was he going to enjoy this? He wondered.

Linda began to play softly on the organ while they waited for the choir director and the organist, and they tried out a few hymns. James did his best to follow the others and to his surprise he was enjoying singing with them. There was one little contralto named Margery, a slight little thing who stood near him while they gathered around Linda at the organ. She gave him a smile as their eyes met. She was not as pretty as Faith and she was far more vivacious, but she somehow reminded him of Faith and he was attracted to her for that reason.

As the others came in and further introductions were made, they took their places and began rehearsal. Margery turned to him as they left the organ.

"Linda has told us about you," she remarked. "She told us what a good voice you had. I'm glad that you're going to be with us. We need more male voices. Most of the boys who can sing are not interested and many who could sing if they tried are afraid to try. I'm glad you're not afraid." She gave him a bright smile.

"I just hope I won't spoil anything while I'm learning," he replied. "You have a mighty big voice for such a small person," he remarked. "It surprised me. I think it is lovely."

"Thank you." Two dimples peeped forth in her smile. "I'm studying hard to improve my voice. I want to major in music next year."

"Thinking of trying for the concert stage?"

"Oh, no!" her eyes widened in swift denial. "I want to use the voice that God gave me for Him in whatever way He might lead me to use it, either on a religious program on the radio or in some evangelistic work or even on the mission field."

"What a waste that would be!" he exclaimed.

Her blue eyes regarded him gravely. "Nothing that is done for God can be a waste," she informed him. "If He should call me to the mission field, I'm sure that I could use my voice for His glory there in a greater way than I could ever use it here."

Their conversation was interrupted by the organ prelude to their anthem. She sat just in front of him and he could hear her rich, deep contralto, which seemed strange coming from such a little thing as she was, so blond and so slight. He was struggling through the number, trying to follow the person next to him, but his mind was not on the music. He was thinking of what this girl had said. What had he gotten into, anyway? Did these young people never think of anything but God? What were they, a group of fanatics? But he knew that

Linda was no fanatic. She was just a sweet, normal girl, but one with a clean mind and a high purpose in life.

He wondered how they could be happy and seemingly so carefree if they had to keep God constantly in mind for fear that they would do something to displease Him. He would feel as if he were under the hand of a slave driver if he had to keep God constantly in mind. How could a girl as pretty as this little creature think of wasting her life in a heathen land, singing to ignorant, dirty natives? Surely she would have to be driven to do a thing like that. She could never go willingly. God must be a severe, merciless taskmaster.

He looked across at Linda singing with her soul in her eyes and with joy radiating from her lovely face and he knew that he was wrong. Love was there, not fear or the knowledge of bondage or compelling servitude. He was the one who was in bondage, he admitted dismally, the bondage of hate. He knew nothing of the lighthearted joyousness of these others singing with their hearts in the song. He suddenly envied them. They possessed something of which he was ignorant and for the first time he wished that he could have what they had.

Linda glanced across at him during an interval and gave him a smile. His heart felt suddenly lighter. She was his friend even though she knew that he was not in the same class with these others. He wondered if they knew that he was different. What would they think and what would they do if they knew the truth?

The pastor came in before they finished and remained a while. They treated him as one of them, talking and joking with him, then he stood nearby arranging the program for the following Sunday services. He was likeable and as he greeted James and made him feel welcome, James felt the charm of his personality. He saw the hidden force within this young preacher that he had seen in Linda and when the minister called Linda aside and talked with her for a while, he could see their eyes meet with an understanding that somehow made him feel as if he were an alien. She had never looked at him that way. He wondered if this young preacher were in love with her. He decided to ask Margery if he were married. He hoped he was.

"Oh, yes," she told him. "His wife is beautiful. She sang with us when they first came here, but she has a son just a few months old, so she has to use her voice to sing lullabies to him."

He uttered a sigh of relief.

When they had finished and were ready to leave, Margery turned to him and said, "I believe you live uptown, don't you? I think Linda said you were over on Prytania."

"Yes, that's right."

He wondered what else Linda had told them about him.

"If you don't have your car, I'd be glad to have you ride with us. We pass right by where you live."

He told her that he didn't have a car and that he would be glad of the lift. In the light of what he knew about all the girls he had met in the past, he wondered if this girl were "making a play" for him. He was soon convinced that he was wrong. There were two girls and two other fellows going in the car.

"You may sit up front with the boys," she told him. "We'll sit back here. I think you'll be getting out first, so you'd better sit on the outside."

The boys did not have much to say on their way but the girls chattered and giggled continually, giving the boys attention now and then by some joking remark. He discovered that they were as normal as any other young people he had met, with one exception. There was nothing suggestive in any of their jokes and smart remarks and they became serious now and then to make some remark that reminded him that they had not forgotten what they were and the One they served.

When the car stopped at his rooming house, they all told him how glad they were that he had joined them and that they looked forward to seeing him Sunday morning.

"If you care to join us at Sunday school, I'll be glad to pick you up," Margery said as he prepared to get out. The car was hers. "We all go down together."

Sunday school! That memory was a horror of his infancy. He surely didn't want to be drawn into that. Not even

Linda could drag him back to that. He thanked Margery but told her that he would not be able to make it for Sunday school.

As they drove away Margery remarked, "There's someone who surely needs the Lord. It's up to us to see that he gets what he needs."

"You did pretty well with him for a starter," teased Phil who was at the wheel. "Just keep up the good work and perhaps you'll win him for your jewel."

"I think Linda can handle him better than I ever could," Margery retorted. "Every time he looked at her while we were there at the organ, it was as if some pagan was looking at the image of his god. There was worship in his eyes."

"What a comparison!" Phil exclaimed. "You surely must have had your eyes on him pretty close to see that worship. Wouldn't Linda feel flattered to know that you compared her to one of those ugly heathen idols."

"Oh, hush! You know what I mean," Margery replied laughing.

As James opened the door to his room he was deep in thought. He had enjoyed being with these young people and he had enjoyed singing. He liked Margery immensely and thought they could become good friends. He liked the boys. They were wholesome and friendly and had made him feel welcome. But he had never been more disturbed in his life. He felt that he was like a drop of poison in a pool of clean, pure water. He was a blot upon a white page. He laughed at his own similes. But the laugh was bitter. It was charged with sorrow. It died upon his lips. How different his life might have been if he had known young people like these years ago. Perhaps he would have looked at what life had dealt him with different eyes and would have accepted the grief and shame with a different attitude. Perhaps he would have looked upon God as they did, with love and reverence, not with anger and bitterness and almost hatred.

Somehow, almost imperceptibly that feeling of near hatred had disappeared. In its place there was a question, a doubt, a longing to really know the truth that Linda believed. He wanted to know, yet he was afraid to know. There was a battle within his soul which made him utterly wretched. How long could this go on, he wondered. Somewhere there would be, there must inevitably be a breaking point. Which would break? His will? His heart? His reason? Only God could tell.

He acknowledged that much as he got into bed and sank wearily back upon his pillow. He was weary in mind and that weariness crept into his very being. He wondered how often Linda prayed. What did Linda say when she prayed? What was prayer anyway? Was it just repeating phrases or sentences in some ritual, as he had repeated a childhood prayer he had learned in Sunday school? He couldn't imagine Linda praying like that. A girl as wise as she would reject such a mechanical means of prayer. He wondered if she ever prayed for him. The thought startled him for he remembered what she had told him long ago after Faith's funeral. She had told him that she would pray that God would keep him from doing whatever it was that had brought him to the city. It was a terrifying thought that she should be talking to God about him. And, so far, that prayer had been answered. What if God had somehow showed her what was in his heart, what that thing was that had brought him here? The thought turned him cold with fear. But that was foolish, he argued, trying to banish the fear. God didn't show a person what another had in his heart. At least he hoped that God didn't.

CHAPTER 22

WHEN SUNDAY MORNING CAME James dreaded going to church. He was fighting a battle with himself. There was something deep within him which told him that he was at the crossroads of his life and he did not know which way he would be going. Not that he had yet given up the search for Martin, but there had entered into his very soul such unrest that at times he felt as if he would lose his reason.

He plunged into his work with such sudden zeal that his fellow workers were surprised. They had noticed his absent-mindedness for some time and they were afraid that he was on his way out. But they observed this sudden change in him and wondered if the boss had had a talk with him and had warned him. He was fighting to keep from thinking.

He knew that if he went to church and heard that preacher give the same type of sermon that he had heard, his battle would be all the greater and he felt that it would be torture. He wished that he could bare his soul to Linda, but he knew that he could not. If he did finally succeed in finding Martin, he would be leaving a plain trail behind him and he would have small chance of escaping the law. He had not even looked at his list lately. He did not want to think of that list just now. He had given up reading murder stories and had turned his attention to other books. He had to read in the evenings when he was alone, for that was the only way he could keep his mind occupied with other things beside his worries.

He marched into the service with the choir feeling nervous and apprehensive. It was his first appearance in the choir robe and he felt conspicuous. He got through the first part of the service better than he had expected and settled back, determined to close his ears to the sermon. He was sitting where he could see Linda and just to look at her seemed to quiet the storm within him. She caught his eye once or twice and gave him a faint smile. He did not know how earnestly she was praying for him that he would hear the whisper of the Spirit's pleading and would open his heart to the Word of God.

As he watched her, trying not to let her see him staring at her, he listened to the sermon in spite of himself. It was a prophetic message, a follow-up on what the preacher had been giving during the weeks at the prayer service. He was giving the congregation some of the signs of the times which gave the Lord's people hope that the end of the age was at hand. He spoke of the upset among the nations, of the alliance which was bringing together the ten nations prophesied in Revelation. He showed them from the Word of God in Daniel how prophecy had been fulfilled, that knowledge would increase and that men would run to and fro as they had never done before. How true it was in this age of the airplane and auto and in the use of atomic power.

He emphasized the fulfilling of prophecy in the increase of sin and immorality, sin which had been so rampant in the days of Noah that God poured out His wrath upon all mankind and wiped out every living creature but those in the Ark. Jesus had said that as it was in the days of Noah, so it would be at the end of the age and surely the world was in that same condition today.

As James listened he was amazed to learn what the Bible contained. Surely it must be the Word of God if so many things had come to pass at the exact time and in the exact

162

manner that had been prophesied, as the preacher explained during his message. He forgot himself in his absorbed interest, but suddenly he was made aware of himself and his own precarious condition when the minister began to impress upon his audience what a terrible thing it would be when God's wrath would again be poured out upon a godless and sinning world. He mentioned only a few highlights in passing, but it was enough to make one think, especially one who was not in the ark of safety, which he described as Jesus Christ. Those in the ark would be carried safely over the waters of judgment to the presence of the Lord, while those who had rejected the gift of salvation would be left to the horrors and sufferings and hopelessness of the reign of the Antichrist.

James was not inclined to believe all that the preacher said, but he was forced to admit that if he believed one part which had been proved so unmistakably, he would have to believe all of it. Horror overwhelmed him at the prospect of being left to go through that Great Tribulation. That was infinitely worse than fleeing from the law or possibly being executed for murder. That would be quick if it came to the worst, but the terrors of the Tribulation would be lingering, while the thought of what might have been would torment one as well as physical torture.

He glanced across at Linda to see how she was taking it. There was a glad light upon her face, no shadow of the horror that filled his being. She was thinking of the rapture and the blessed privilege of being in the presence of her Lord. He realized that and the longing to have what she had and to be like her in faith and assurance grew stronger within him.

When the service was over he felt a wave of relief. He had never had such an experience, such a battle of emotions, and he felt weak and exhausted as the result. He met Linda as they came out of the choir rooms after removing their robes.

"Did you listen this morning or were you wandering?" she asked.

"I listened," he admitted.

"It was a compelling and thrilling message," she remarked. "One to make a person think and to be glad that he is safe in the Lord. I shall be looking for you tonight. You'll be here, won't you?"

"Yes, I'll be here," he assured her.

How could he stay away when she looked at him like that and when she said she would be looking for him?

Margery offered to take him home so he went with them. They were serious this morning. There were no jokes and no giggles. They discussed the sermon and he could see that it had made a deep impression upon them.

"That was a wonderful message," Margery remarked. "I'm learning more about the Bible under Dr. Sawyer than I ever knew before."

"Boy! Am I glad that I'm saved!" Phil exclaimed. "If I weren't, I think I'd have gotten down on my knees right there this morning and asked God to save me. What a fool I was to wait so long to accept the Lord. I feel guilty when I think of all the years I wasted when I could have been serving Him."

"If the Lord should come today, I'm afraid I'd have very little to show that I have done for Him," Margery sighed.

"You said it," one of the other boys replied. "We're all selfish with our time and our talents. We forget that someone might be just waiting for us to witness to him and lead him to the Lord."

James was silent and he felt that surely they must know why. He hoped that they wouldn't guess that he did not have what they had, that sense of security and their faith in God. He didn't want them to begin on him. He didn't know that they knew exactly what he needed. Their spiritual perception had told them in the beginning that he was not a Christian. But they had tact enough not to say anything that would embarrass him or perhaps drive him away. They were leaving him to Linda as Margery had suggested.

He was so nervous when he had eaten and gone back to his room that he could not stay there, yet when he went outside there was no place he wanted to go. He wished that he could talk to Linda, yet he feared that she would only upset him more. She would make him want to accept the Lord and he knew that he could not do that.

He walked the streets for a while, then returned to his room and tried to read. His mind would not stay on what he was reading. The memory of that sermon and what those young people said kept revolving in a whirl through his thoughts. Suddenly he got up and went to his desk where the ominous list was. He took it out and tore it to shreds. When the last fragment had dropped into the wastebasket it was as if a great load had rolled from him. His old man of the sea had loosened his hold, or so he thought just then. He went back to his chair and picked up the paper which he had just bought.

The next morning he went to work with a lighter heart than he had had in years. The dread search for Martin was over. Then something happened in which James could have seen Satan's hand if he had been familiar with the way Satan worked in human lives. He was not willing to let his victim go so easily.

Someone came into the office for a conference with the manager about some goods that were to be shipped to South America. James was busy on the other side of the room when the man came in and he did not notice him until the man spoke.

"Tell Mr. Gunther that Thomas Martin is here to keep our appointment," the man told a girl in answer to her question.

James heard the name and raised his head. With startled, wide eyes he looked at the man. Then his heart began a mad pounding. This Thomas Martin was an almost exact duplicate of the picture he had carried with him for so long. The same heavy face, the same hair and the eyes, even at that distance had the same look. It must be the man he sought. And just when he had torn up the list and given up the search.

As he watched the man in the brief time he had, there raged through him all the hatred that he had carried for so long. This man, looking so prosperous, had lived in comfort and peace through the years, while his victims had suffered much. Well, he would not live much longer to enjoy his ill-gotten fortune. He would pay the penalty and suffer torture of mind and body before his evil life was snuffed out.

All the memory of the two sermons James had heard was wiped out. All the longing to be like those others was gone. In its place hate reared its ugly head, and revenge turned his heart to bitterness once more.

He could scarcely wait until the man had left until he went into the manager's office to inquire about him. He gave as an excuse that this Martin was an old friend of the family and he wanted the opportunity to meet him and have a talk with him. He got the man's address and tried to concentrate on his work until closing time, but he found it difficult, almost impossible.

On the way home he tried to formulate some plan. He had thought of a hundred plans in the past but none of them satisfied him. He had thought that he would manage when the time came. But now the time was here and there was little time to think of any plan. This man was going to South America in a few days. He was stopping at a downtown hotel. It would be difficult to carry out any of the plans he had thought about, but he must do the deed before the man left and was lost to him forever.

He tried to eat his dinner but he had no appetite and he returned to his room and tried to think of some plan. He could not just go in and kill the man after telling him why he was going to die. That would be too easy. He wanted the man to suffer. But first he must meet him and have a talk with him to be sure that he was the right man. There was no time to lose, so he decided to go at once to the hotel and have an interview with him. He would give some excuse about the shipment. He knew little about that, but he thought that he could make up some lie while he was getting the information he needed.

He was relieved when he phoned and found Martin in his room. He asked if he might see him and went up immediately when he was told that he could.

The moment he saw this Martin he knew that he was not

the man he sought. He had not thought of this before, for the likeness to that picture had been so perfect that it had given him a shock. Now he realized with an even greater shock that the man he sought would be much older. The years would be bound to make a difference. He would no longer be as young a man as this Thomas Martin was.

Though he was sure that he had made a mistake, he knew he would have to go through with his visit, since he had already come to the man's room. He gave the flimsy excuse that he thought he might be able to give him some further help with the shipment or with his baggage. He intimated that the manager had sent him there to see if he could be of assistance.

Martin thanked him but told him that he needed nothing. He invited James to sit down and have a little visit since he had gone to this trouble to help him. James accepted his invitation. He led the man to talk about his past and where he had lived, and before he left there was no doubt in his mind that this was not the Martin he sought. This man had lived in South America the greater part of his life. He had never been west. James knew that he was telling the truth.

When he finally left he felt that the load was again lifted from him. But he was down in the depths nevertheless. He knew, from the upsurge of that old hatred and the quick decision to take revenge upon this possible victim, that the root of it was still there like a poison that could not be removed. He felt that he was doomed. How could he ever hope to have the peace of God in his heart when that remained as a barrier? Surely there was no hope for him.

CHAPTER 23

JAMES DECIDED THAT he would have to have a talk with Linda. He would have to confess at least a part of the reason for the burden that was growing impossible to bear. If she could not help him, he did not know what he would do. He couldn't go on any longer in this unhappy situation. He couldn't sleep and he couldn't eat.

It didn't make him any happier when he noticed how attentive one of the older boys was to Linda. He could see that the fellow was in love with her. It spoke from his eyes whenever James saw him looking at her. This young man, Jack Stoddard, had been less friendly than any of the others when James first joined the choir. He recalled the watchful eye of the fellow whenever he saw James talking to Linda. Now he realized that Jack was jealous of the attention Linda paid him. James saw them leave together after choir practice and he wondered if they were going to Linda's or whether they were going somewhere for a snack.

He knew that Linda was popular with all of them but that she seemed to have no favorites. However, it was quite evident now that Jack seemed to be the one she was interested in. James wondered just how far that interest went. The others had noticed it, too, and they remarked about it one evening on their way home.

"Jack surely has fallen for Linda in a big way," Margery remarked.

"Who wouldn't?" Phil replied. "She's such a peach that any fellow would fall for her if he thought there was a chance for him."

"Jack doesn't seem to know that others have tried before he came to melt that heart of stone," another boy remarked. "He thinks that because she has bent over backwards to make him feel at home with us, he can make some headway with her. He's doomed to have a fall. I don't think she even has a thought about falling in love with anyone."

"I think you're wrong," Margery said. "I think she likes him a lot. They go out together more often than she has ever been with any other fellow."

"Time will tell," Phil replied. "In the meantime, how about a root beer float?"

All except James agreed that it would be a good idea, so they left him off near his room and he went on alone, thinking of what they had said about Linda. This Jack must be a new member. And he mistook Linda's kindness for heart interest. Or was it just kindness on her part? He hoped it was. The next day he phoned her and asked if he might come to see her.

"I need your advice," he told her. "I need you terribly. I'm having a terrific struggle with myself and if I can only have a talk with you, I'm sure that you can help me."

"I was just thinking of you," she told him. "How about coming out to dinner tomorrow evening? I want you to meet my mother. Dad is too sick to eat with us, but Mother is anxious to meet you. She has heard you sing and she thinks you have a good voice. Would you care to come?"

"Would I!" he exclaimed. "It's good of you to ask."

His spirits soared. The hours dragged by until time for him to start for her home. She met him with her usual smile and they went almost at once to the dining room where Mrs. Martinez was waiting for them. Linda introduced him to her mother and she made him feel most welcome as they sat down to the meal.

They bowed their heads and he followed after a moment of embarrassment, for he had been about to speak. Mrs. Martinez returned thanks in a few well-chosen words which James felt came from her heart. Then she spoke to him.

"I've heard you and Linda singing, and you can't imagine how well your voices blend. I do love those old hymns."

"I'm sorry I've never had the opportunity to learn them," James replied. "I think they are beautiful and I love to sing them. I'm enjoying singing with the choir, though I'm afraid I'm not much help."

"I'm sure you are," she remarked graciously. "I miss going to church, but Mr. Martinez has become so melancholy that I hate to leave him alone."

They carried on a casual conversation as they ate. The meal was delicious and James remarked about it.

"This is the first home cooked meal that I've eaten in months," he told them. "And it's just about the best I ever ate."

"You can thank Linda for that. She's a fine cook," her mother said with a fond smile at her daughter.

"I had a good teacher," Linda told him. "Mother did all the cooking until Dad became worse, so I'm just a substitute."

When the meal was finished Mrs. Martinez excused herself, saying that she must go to her husband.

"That means that you'll have to help me with the dishes," Linda told him. "Think you can stand it?"

"I'm sure I can. I used to help Mother, but I'll confess that I broke a lot of china."

"I'll take the risk." She smiled and led the way to the kitchen. "As soon as we finish, we'll have that talk, but just now I must concentrate on these dishes and pots."

Before they had finished the bell rang. Linda answered it and James heard Jack's voice. He was angry and disappointed. This was no time for him to come barging in and spoiling his evening.

Jack followed Linda into the kitchen. A brief look of

animosity shot from his eyes when he saw James, then he smiled engagingly.

"I see you're training some new kitchen help," he remarked.

"He doesn't need training. He's already an expert," Linda told him. "Get a towel and pitch in, so we'll get through that much sooner."

"I hope you'll forgive me for crashing in like this," Jack said as they finished and went into the living room. "I had something I wanted to discuss with you and it won't keep until tomorrow."

James was inclined to doubt that and his anger increased. Linda did her best to handle the difficult situation, for she knew how desperately James wanted to talk with her, but it seemed that Jack was determined not to leave, so, after a while, when the conversation became rather strained and James saw that Jack had no intention of leaving, he thanked her for inviting him and then left. He raged inwardly all the way home.

At choir practice he still bore a grudge against Jack for his unmannerly conduct and he sat glum and silent during the time when they waited for the others to come. Linda saw and she was disturbed. She knew that James was going through a time of spiritual struggle. Her own spiritual insight told her that and her heart cried out to God that he might be a victor. She had looked forward to talking with him for she felt that this was an answer to prayer. How wonderful it would be if she could lead him to the Lord! Then she would not feel so unhappy because she could not help loving him. She had seen something in his eyes now and then when she had caught him looking at her that told her he was interested. Perhaps someday she might be able to take the place in his heart that Faith had left vacant.

When choir practice was over, she stopped him as he was about to join Margery and the others.

"Would you like to go home with me and have that talk?" she asked.

"Oh, yes, I would!" he exclaimed.

He hurried out to tell the group that he wouldn't be going with them. When he returned he saw Linda and Jack talking alone. Jack was holding her hand and talking earnestly. He turned in surprise when he heard James approaching and his gaze was none too friendly.

"I thought you were gone," he remarked as he released Linda's hand.

"Evidently," James retorted curtly.

That little scene wakened a new emotion with him, raging jealousy that made him want to crash his fist into Jack's face.

"Let's be going," Linda said to James. "Good night, Jack."

She gave him a smile and she and James went out together following Jack who strode rapidly and angrily ahead of them.

"I'm sorry if I interrupted something that I shouldn't have," James remarked as they left the church.

"I'm glad you did," she told him. "Jack was getting out of hand. I think he took too much for granted."

Her answer boosted his spirits somewhat, but he was still moody and silent as they walked the short distance to her home. He followed her up the steps and stood beside her while she unlocked the door. When she opened the door, she turned to him with a smile.

"Now we can have that talk. I do so want to help you and see you happy."

Suddenly, on a wild, uncontrollable impulse, entirely unpremeditated, he caught her in his arms and held her close, almost brutally close, then he kissed her.

For a moment she remained passive in his arms and her lips answered his while joy swept through her at the touch of his lips, then swift anger took its place. She pushed him violently from her.

"How dare you do that?" she cried. Her eyes flashed fire in the light from the living room.

He hung his head in embarrassment.

"I'm sorry," he murmured. "I just couldn't help it.

You're so beautiful. And I love you!" he blurted out. "I love you! I just couldn't help it. Please forgive me. I didn't know I was going to do it."

For a moment she said nothing. She was trying to control her voice. Then she said quietly and what she hoped was calmly, "I forgive you, but I think you had better go. Good night."

She turned and went inside and closed the door without looking back.

For a moment he stood staring at the closed door, then he turned and stumbled away in the darkness, feeling that he had lost his last chance for the hope of peace.

As he stood waiting for the bus he tried to calm his troubled mind and clear his confused thoughts. He had had no idea of kissing her and he was thoroughly ashamed of himself for hurting her, yet he was not sorry that he had kissed her. He knew now that he had been in love with her almost from the time of Faith's funeral. Even while he had been brokenhearted over Faith's death, Linda's sweet sympathy that had been balm to his heart had been the beginning. When he had been so deep within his grief and loneliness, he knew now that it was love for Linda that had made him turn to her and it was love for her that had taken him through the agonizing days that were torture. How he could be in love with the memory of one girl, keeping her image in his heart and at the same time be in love with another girl, he did not try to understand. He just knew that it was so. But now he had lost even the faint hope of winning her love.

How could someone like himself, he thought disconsolately, dare hope that a girl like Linda could ever fall in love with him? He had nothing to offer and others had much. No matter, he had lost his chance and only loneliness and the torture of conflict remained. He had indeed been a fool. Where could he turn now?

CHAPTER 24

LINDA DID NOT LOOK BACK at James when she told him good night because she did not want him to see the tears that were streaming down her face. She went to her room hoping that her mother would not hear her, for she did not want her mother to see those tears either. She knew that she could not explain them. She could scarcely explain to herself. She was conscious of her weakness and of the strength of her love and she was ashamed because she had responded so willingly to his kiss. She had wanted him to kiss her and she had wanted to remain in his arms, though she felt that it was not right that she should want to. She could not control her love, for she had tried and failed, and she realized sadly that she could not control the joy that shot through her at the memory of that kiss. She was angry with herself for her weakness.

When she knelt by her bed she scarcely knew what to pray. She wanted the love of this unknown one who had come into her life under such unusual circumstances, yet she knew that as a Christian she had no right to that love. If she could not overcome it, she should at least be strong enough not to let it control her better judgment. She prayed earnestly that James would become a Christian, but even as she prayed, the humiliating knowledge lay within her that she wanted him to become a Christian first of all so that she could love him without feeling guilty. She had to be honest with God, for she knew that He could see within her heart. She prayed for guidance and for strength.

There was one comforting thought as she wept and prayed. She had been concerned about this man's soul before she fell in love with him. That gave her only small comfort, but it was better than nothing.

James did not appear for choir practice and he was not at church on Sunday. The next week he was still absent and the others wondered what had happened to him. Linda felt guilty and miserable. She knew why he did not come and she became more worried as the third week passed and he did not appear. She was more concerned about his spiritual welfare than anything else. She knew that he had sought her because he was in some deep distress and she had not given him the comfort and help that he felt she could give him. She decided that she would have to do something about it. She wrote him a note, inviting him to dinner again and assuring him that if he still wanted to talk to her about some problem, there would be no interruption this time.

He read the note over and over, then pressed it to his lips. He felt like a condemned prisoner who had just received a pardon. He went to the phone at once and thanked her for the note and told her how glad he would be to accept her invitation.

Mrs. Martinez was upstairs when he arrived and dinner was not quite ready, so they sat in the living room for a little while.

"I hope that I'm forgiven," he said humbly as they sat down.

"I told you that you were forgiven," she said gently, "but in the future, let's keep our relationship on a strictly friendly basis."

"I'll do whatever you say, but just let me keep on seeing you."

Just then Mrs. Martinez came in and they went into the

dining room. The meal was enjoyable and the conversation interesting, but casual. James asked about Mr. Martinez and his wife told him that he was just about the same.

"The doctor says his mental condition is what keeps him from improving. He seems to have sunk into a state of melancholy and nothing that we can do will bring him out of it. It has been coming on for a long time, but lately it has become much worse. I can't account for it and I'm worried about him."

James again expressed his sympathy.

When the dishes were finished and they were alone, Linda said, "Now for the problem. What is it?"

"It's more than a problem," he said heavily. "I've been so upset that I almost feel like ending it all."

"That would only make matters worse," she reminded him.

"At least I'd be out of my misery," he sighed.

"No, you'd be in more misery than you could ever imagine. Death is a horrible thing to a person without Christ. Will you let me say something? I don't want to preach or annoy you. I want to help you. Christ is the only answer to your problem, to all of them, whatever they might be. He is the only One who can help you solve them and give you peace of mind and heart, because you can lay all of your troubles upon Him and He will help you bear them or take them away entirely. Why not give Him a chance?"

"I've come to the place where I wish I could." He uttered a sigh that was almost a groan. "You know that I didn't believe, even when Faith showed such a change in her life. I didn't want to believe because I knew that there was no hope for me even if I did want to believe."

"How can you think that there is no hope?" she asked. "There is hope for everyone who will come to the Lord and ask for forgiveness."

"You don't understand," he said miserably as he rubbed his hands together nervously. "I couldn't ask God to forgive my sin when there was something that I knew that I was going to do which would keep Him from forgiving me."

"You mentioned that once and I prayed about it, that God would keep you from doing it, for I felt that it would keep you from Him. Tell me about it if it will help."

He raised his head and looked at her with eyes that were dark with suffering and doubt. And fear — fear that when she heard, she would turn from him in horror.

"I came to New Orleans to kill a man," he said slowly. "I spent my spare time here until Faith's death trying to find him. I knew that if I did find him, no matter how long it took, I would kill him as I would kill a mad dog. I haven't found him yet."

"I thank God for that," she said earnestly. "I believe that it was an answer to my prayer. It would be a terrible thing for you to commit murder as you planned to do. I'm sure that God kept you from doing that."

"But I still have hate in my heart for this man and I know that if I should find him even now, I would kill him if I could."

"But would that help you in any way?" she asked.

"I'd at least make him suffer for what he did to my life and to those I loved. I'd like to make him suffer just as much and as long as he made my mother and father suffer. And for what he did to my life. I've hated him ever since I was small. I've carried that hate in my heart all these years and it's still there now."

"God's Word says 'Vengeance is mine, I will repay,'" she quoted. "His Word is true, whether you believe it or not, James. Why not leave it to Him?"

A sudden light leaped into his eyes. It was the first time she had ever called him by his given name and even in this trying moment, when his soul was in such turmoil, a glimmer of joy shot through him.

"I wasn't willing to wait for God to do anything about it. I didn't even know that He would care. Just recently I made up my mind that I'd give up looking for him. I thought I'd forget the whole thing, but that hate is still in my heart and I can have no peace day or night."

"God can wipe that hate out of your heart," she told

177

him. "When His love fills your heart there is no room for hate. You may think that that is impossible, but it isn't. A change takes place in your life and in your heart and even in your thoughts, in such an imperceptible yet miraculous way that before you realize it, you know you are a new creature in Christ Jesus."

He looked at her desperately.

"Do you think that it could happen to me? I've got to have peace!" he cried in an agonized voice. "This struggle I'm going through is torture."

"It could and it can happen to you," she assured him. "If you will just surrender your will and your doubts to Him and ask for that peace, He will give it to you in the same way that He gave it to Faith and that He gave it to me."

"I want to believe! I want to," he said in a voice that trembled.

"If you want to, you can receive it tonight. If you want me to, I shall pray with you and for you, that God will help you to open your heart and receive Christ as your Saviour this very hour."

He stared at her aghast. He was not quite ready for such a drastic step. "Tonight? Now?" he asked

"If that is what you want. But you have to want to be saved. If you do it just to please me or because you hate to refuse what I've offered to do, you will receive nothing and you'll only be wasting my time and yours, but if you really want what you say you do, there is nothing to keep you from receiving it but you and your will."

He looked at her a while in silence and there was such desperate longing in his eyes that her own eyes filled with tears.

"I want it," he said.

"Then will you kneel with me?"

He nodded and they knelt together. She prayed a prayer such as he had never heard, one which brought unwilling tears to his eyes while sobs finally shook him as he heard her pleading with the Lord for his understanding and his faith and willingness to yield his life to the Lord.

When she had finished, she asked him if he would be willing to ask the Lord to forgive him if she would tell him what to say. He said that he was willing. In a voice muffled by sobs, he repeated the words she gave him, then when he had finished, she asked him if he believed that God had forgiven him and saved him.

"I don't know," he faltered. "I hope so."

"But you must believe," she told him. "When you asked the Lord to forgive you and save you, you did all that any person can do. Jesus did it all when He shed His blood on Calvary. Now if you did your part you must believe that God did His part when you asked Him. Will you say that you believe and trust Him?"

He raised his head and smiled through his tears.

"I get it. That's what you told Faith. I remember it now. I do believe. It isn't going to be easy to go on, for I know that old hate will rise up within me, but I'm going to do my best to kill it."

"Don't let it bother you. Just let God take care of it," she said as they rose from their knees.

"You must think me an awful baby," he remarked as he wiped his eyes.

"No I don't. I'm glad for those tears and I know that they rejoiced the heart of God. When tears come then I know something has really reached the heart."

"How can I ever thank you for what you have done for me?" he asked.

"By going on with the Lord. It may not be easy, but God will help you if you'll only remember to ask Him day by day. And by coming back to the choir," she added with a smile as she wiped her own tears away.

"I'll be there," he promised.

When he left her the world seemed a different place. Gone was the torture of the struggle and gone was the burden. He knew that he had not yet conquered the hate that had controlled his life but he knew that it would fade, for he had given up any idea of trying to find his victim. The only blot upon his new joy was the memory of Linda's words. They must keep their relationship upon a friendly footing. How could he when he loved her more now than ever?

The next few days seemed strange and unreal to him. After the storm that had raged within him there was peace at last, a peace that he could scarcely believe because it seemed impossible. There was an emptiness within him as he realized that the search to which he had dedicated his life was over, but it was a blessed emptiness. The world seemed different even though he was still lonely and even though he felt he could never dare hope that Linda would love him. But there was no despair in that loneliness.

He saw those in the office and in the little restaurant with new eyes. He felt a friendliness toward them that he had never felt before. He wanted to smile at them and seek their friendship.

This change which came so imperceptibly made him aware that a miracle had really happened to him within his soul and that he was not the same person he had been. Love had entered his heart, not the kind of love he felt for Linda, but what she called the love of God. He knew that he had much to learn, but he was grateful for the essential foundational fact that he believed in the love of God and he knew that because Christ had died for his sins he was a saved soul, for he had accepted Christ's gift of salvation.

Linda was so happy that she could scarcely believe it was real. She had prayed earnestly for this and now that it had happened and her prayers had been answered, life would be perfect for her but for one thing. Her father was not a Christian. But if God could change James' hardened, hate-filled heart, He could surely change her father's heart and save his soul before it was too late.

Mr. Martinez seemed to be growing steadily weaker and the doctor told them after his last visit that unless some changes took place in his mental attitude, it would only be a question of time. Medical science had done all that was possible. He did not seem to want to live. Linda and her mother couldn't understand it. He had everything to live for. This knowledge made Linda's heart ache, but her faith was still strong and she would not give up hope for him.

She lost no time in telling the choir that James had accepted Christ. She knew that they were interested and that some of them had been praying for him. He arrived just a few minutes after she had told them and they gave him such a warmhearted greeting that he was overwhelmed.

"We're glad that you've accepted the Lord," Margery told him when they were seated in their places. "Now you are really one of us."

"Then you knew I wasn't a Christian before?" he asked.

"Sure we did. No one told us, but we just knew. One can usually tell by the way a person reacts when others talk about the Lord whether that person really loves Him or not."

When they were ready to leave, James asked Linda if he might walk home with her and she accepted his offer. There was no longer any reason for her to deny his request to see her more often. It had been self-denial on her part when she had refused him before.

"I have much to learn," James said when they were on their way. "I do wish that you could teach me. I don't know a thing about the Bible and I don't know much about how a Christian should live. But I'm anxious to know. These past few days have been the most wonderful days of my life."

"I'm glad," she responded with a happy smile. "I'll do what I can to teach you, but if you really want to know something more about the Bible, why not come to Sunday school?"

"Sunday school!" he echoed in disappointed tones. "I was hoping that you could give me a little help."

She smiled in the darkness as she replied, "You could join my class. Most of the choir members belong. I'd love to have you join us."

"Oh! That's different. I'll surely come."

His sudden enthusiasm made them both laugh.

When he was ready to leave, he held her hand for a

moment as she extended it and said earnestly, "I'm grateful to you and to the Lord for giving me the privilege of knowing you."

He raised her hand to his lips and kissed it, then he left her.

She stood watching him until he disappeared and there was a song in her heart, a little new song that needed no accompaniment except the beating of that glad heart.

CHAPTER 25

JAMES WAS SURE that he would enjoy attending Sunday school since Linda was the teacher, but as time passed a new struggle arose. He could not keep his mind on the lesson for thinking of Linda. She had given him the ultimatum that their relationship must be on a friendly basis alone and he felt that he could no longer continue on that basis. His love for her was something that he could not control and each time they were together he realized how impossible it would be for him to continue as just a friend. He finally decided that it would be best for him to go away. If he were where he could not see her and long for her, perhaps he would forget her. At least he would not be as unhappy as he was now. Seeing her and being near her and knowing that she could never be his took away some of the newfound joy in his salvation.

He had not yet learned the power of prayer and he felt that he did not know how to really pray, but when he knelt each morning and evening as Linda had suggested, he poured out his heart in supplication for her love. There was no need for him to be taught how to pray for this, for it was the cry of his heart to the God in whose power he believed.

One evening as they walked home after the service, he asked if he might come in for a few minutes.

"I have something I want to tell you," he said. "I've come to a decision and I want you to know what it is."

She saw the serious look on his face and wondered what the decision was. They went inside and she sat as usual on the couch beside him.

"I've decided to go away," he said, coming to the subject at once.

"To go away!" she echoed. "Where are you going?"

"I don't know," he admitted. "Just away."

"Why this sudden decision to go away?" She tried to hide the anxiety and disappointment in her voice.

"I want to get away from here so that I can have some peace of mind."

"But I thought you were happy here since you've accepted the Lord. Has anyone done anything to hurt you?"

"No. I've been happier here since I was saved than I've ever been in my life, but I just can't stand any longer to be near you and to know that I can never have your love."

She stared at him with wide eyes for a moment, then said in a low voice in a tone which he mistook for sympathy, but which was so charged with joy that she could scarcely control it, "Oh! I didn't know you really cared."

"But I do," he declared. His eyes were full of pain as he looked at her. "I love you so much that it's torture to be near you and to know that you can never be anything but a friend. That's why I think I should go away somewhere where I can try to forget you. I know I never shall, though, for I love you, Linda, very much."

She smiled a tremulous little smile and said in tones throbbing with joy, "If that's the reason, you won't have to go away, James, my dear. We can be more than friends if that is what you wish."

He gulped and stared, then as she continued to smile, he stammered, "Are you trying to tell me that you can learn to love me?"

"I learned that long ago, even before you did, I'm afraid."

"But you said we could only be friends," he stammered.

"That was because you were not a Christian and I could never let myself yield to that love unless you were. It's different now."

He stared at her a moment, still not able to believe, then light broke through and with a smothered cry he held out his arms to her.

"Linda! Oh, Linda!" he cried as he held her close, then his lips met hers.

This time her lips answered his and there was no reproach, only glad surrender.

"I can't believe it, but how I thank God for answered prayer," he murmured when there was time for speech.

"Call me Jimmie, won't you?" he asked presently. "I want to hear it from your lips."

"I don't feel that I should," she demurred. "That was Faith's special name for you. I would feel that I was taking something that belonged to her."

"She told me that you would take her place and that I would love you as much as she did. I think she would be happy if she knew and somehow I think she would be willing for you to call me by her own special name for me."

"If that's what you wish, Jimmie," she whispered as she rested within his arms.

For them time had ceased to exist, for they had entered a realm where nothing but love was real.

"I'll never be able to give you the things you've been used to if you marry me, at least not for a long time," he told her presently. "Would you be satisfied with the little I could afford? I don't want to wait for you until I do have more."

"I'll be satisfied with just having you," she told him. "It will be fun making a little go a long way and you'll be surprised how well I can do that."

"Let's not tell anyone just now but Mother and Dad," she suggested. "I want to wait a while and see how Dad gets along. I couldn't leave Mother alone now when he is so ill."

"Please don't keep me waiting too long," he begged.

"I've wasted too much time already in being unhappy. I want to begin to live this new life with you by my side helping me to live it in the right way."

When he came back the next evening Linda met him with a worried light in her eyes.

"It's Dad," she told him. "When I told him about us he was upset and he's been in a terrible state ever since. Mother says it's because he doesn't want to lose me. She said that perhaps if you would meet him and he would get to know you, he wouldn't be so upset. You might tell him that you wouldn't take me away until he gets well."

"I'll hate to tell him that, but I'll do it if you think it will help him," he told her. "I've been wanting to meet him. I'm afraid that if he doesn't want to give you up, whatever I may say won't help much."

"Let's go and see," and she led the way upstairs.

"Dad, this is James," she said. "I want you two to get acquainted. I'll leave you together for a little while. You can call me if you need me."

The two men looked at each other silently for a few moments. Mr. Martinez was even more emaciated than James had imagined. His black eyes shone like two pinpoints of steel as he continued to stare at James. There was a look of wretchedness in them, along with a look of animosity that puzzled James. Presently Mr. Martinez spoke in a deep, husky voice.

"So you are James Thornton. Don't you know that you can never marry my daughter?"

James scarcely heard what the man said. His attention was focused upon a framed photo on the dresser nearby. As he stared at the picture horror filled him and his heart began a mad pounding. His face turned deathly pale and he held on to the bedpost where he stood. Then he turned to the man on the bed and his eyes were cold and hard.

"You are Thomas Martin," he said slowly.

Each word seemed like a leaden weight dropping from stiff lips.

"I was Thomas Martin."

The words were uttered in a voice that was dead and cold. They sounded as if they had come from someone who had been struggling for a long while and had at last given up the struggle.

"So you changed your name. That's why I couldn't find you."

Martinez shook his head weakly.

"No. I only shortened it. My name is Edwin Thomas Martinez."

"I came to this city to find you and kill you," James cried. "If I had found you just a little while ago, I would have killed you as I would have killed a mad dog. You haven't deserved to live all these years when it was you who caused the death of my father in prison and who broke my mother's heart and caused her death. I've looked for you for months. I wanted to make you suffer as much as I could before I killed you in return for all you made us suffer."

"Can't you see that I've suffered more than death?" Martinez asked in a voice grown suddenly weak. "I've suffered the tortures of mind and body ever since that time of weakness when I let my friend pay the penalty for my crime. I've never had a moment of peace since. That's what has brought me to where I am now. The doctor says I'm dying because I no longer have the will to live. That's true. I can't carry the burden any longer. I've kept it from my wife and daughter and it's been slowly killing me."

He paused a moment for lack of strength while James watched him with eyes that flashed with anger and accusation.

"If it was revenge that brought you here to look for me, then you should be satisfied. You've had your revenge. Just look at me."

"But you're still living," James uttered through white lips, "while they are dead. You wrecked my whole life, for after my father died, my life was full of hate, hate for you and the determination to find you and kill you. That one purpose has dominated my whole life."

"It need not dominate it any longer," the sick man said,

"for I'll soon be dead and you will have had your revenge."

"But you'll die a natural death. You don't deserve that."

"At least it will save you from being hanged for my murder," Martinez retorted bitterly. "Now you see why you can never marry Linda. She'll have to know the truth now. I'll give you the privilege of telling her what a scoundrel her father is. Perhaps you may get some satisfaction out of that."

"Do you think I could get any satisfaction from hurting her? I love her! It's up to you to tell her if you want to. I'm leaving."

He left the room and met Linda on the stairway. Mrs. Martinez came up and stood beside her.

"We couldn't help but hear," Linda explained, "for the door was open."

Her face was white and her eyes were full of pain.

"I'm sorry," he replied. "I'll be going. Good night."

"Don't go, Jimmie," Linda said taking hold of his hand and detaining him. "I must talk to you. Don't go like this."

"I have to," he said as he gently released his hand. "I've got to get away and be alone. Please don't ask me to stay."

She let him go while tears filled her eyes. The door closed behind him and she and her mother went into her father's room.

"I heard you out there on the steps," he told them as they came in. "I'm glad you heard it all. Now I won't have to tell you. I'm glad that at last you know. It's been hell on earth all these years, keeping this weight on my conscience. I don't see now how I've lived through it all this time. Now I can die in peace."

He sighed heavily and closed his eyes as if he were utterly exhausted.

"You're not going to die, Daddy," Linda said as she knelt by the bed and took his hand in hers. "You're not ready to die. Now that this weight has been lifted from your heart you can confess to the Lord and He will forgive you and save your soul. Now I know why you wouldn't let us talk to you about the Lord. You knew that if you asked Him to forgive you, you would have to confess this thing that you have kept in your heart all this time. Isn't that the reason?''

He nodded while tears trickled slowly from under his closed lids.

"I've wanted peace in my heart for a long, long while. But, my dear, if I confess to God, I'll have to confess to the law and pay the penalty for my crime. What about that?''

"If that is what you must do, then you will have to do it," she told him. "However, that was long ago and the case has been closed for many years, so legally it may not be necessary. I suppose it's up to James whether or not he wants the case reopened.''

"From the way he looked and spoke, I think he'd be glad to do anything that would make me suffer more than I have," her father replied.

"I don't think so, Dad. He loves me and he loves the Lord. When he has had time to get over this shock, I'm sure that he will want to do what is right, in spite of what he has felt all these years.''

"Pray for me, Linda," her father begged. "I've wanted that, but I dared not ask for it.''

She and her mother knelt beside the bed and they prayed with him and for him and before they left the room another soul had been born into the family of God.

James left the house and wandered through the darkness out to the lake front. He sat for a long time upon the sea wall where the waves dashed against the stone steps, whipped by a stiff breeze. His soul was in torment again. He was filled with anguish because the hate which he had thought was dead had risen to life within him when he had seen that photograph. He did not know how to combat this thing which had risen to life like a monster which had been seemingly killed, but which had only been laid low for a while.

The future looked Stygian black to him. How could he marry Linda with this thing between them? He couldn't pray and he couldn't think straight. Finally he returned to his room. He tossed through a sleepless night and went to work with a heavy heart and a sense of defeat. He felt that he had failed God and that God had cast him off because he was no longer worthy of belonging to Him.

That evening Linda called him and asked him to come out to her home. He was surprised to think that she still wanted to see him after what she knew and what she had heard him say to her father.

When he came and she met him at the door, she held up her lips for his kiss and he took her in his arms and held her close.

"I was afraid you would never want to see me again," he told her. "I've failed God and I'm afraid I've failed you. I had hate in my heart when I thought that it was all gone."

"We all fail God at times. That's because we're weak and the old nature is still strong within us. That doesn't excuse us, but God will forgive us when we repent and ask Him to forgive."

"But I haven't asked Him," he said. "I didn't have the courage. I felt that I didn't deserve forgiveness after the way I felt and what I said to your father."

"None of us deserve His forgiveness, but He forgives just the same. That's what makes Him so wonderful. I wish you could know how abjectly Dad repented last night. You may not realize it, but you have had your revenge many times over, Jimmie. If you had lived with him during these years, you would know that I speak the truth. He suffered more than death. He wants to see you and to beg you to forgive him for all the suffering he has caused you and your parents. Will you see him? Can you forgive him?"

"I don't know," he answered slowly. "Perhaps if I ask the Lord to forgive me for having this hate in my heart, He will take it away and then I'll know what I can do. It will be terribly hard. He wrecked the lives of all three of us."

"I know. I know what you have suffered, but we have suffered, too, all three of us. That's what sin does. It not only affects the one who sins, but it affects those who belong to that one. Will you pray with me?"

"Of course. That's what I want."

They prayed together. Linda asked the Lord to give him grace enough to know what forgiveness was and James prayed for forgiveness for himself and for the Lord to take away guilt from his heart once and for all. When they arose from their knees, she looked at him through her tears.

"Now, since God, for Christ's sake, has forgiven you, can't you, for my sake, forgive Dad?" she asked.

"I'll try," he said and managed a smile.

Together they went to the sick man's room.

"Dad, here is James," she said.

James stood by the bed and waited for Mr. Martinez to speak. He held out a thin, trembling hand to James and said, "Can you find it in your heart to forgive me for the great wrong I did to you? God has forgiven me, now will you?"

James' hand trembled as he clasped the hand extended to him and in his eyes were tears of which he was not ashamed as he spoke.

"If God can forgive you, who am I to say that I will not? I thank Him that He has forgiven me."

For a moment there was silence while the two kept their hands clasped, then a sob tore itself from Linda's throat. Mrs. Martinez was weeping silently.

"Do you still want to marry my daughter?" Mr. Martinez asked.

"More than anything else in the world," James said fervently.

"Then let's get it over soon, so that we can all be as happy as we would like to be. I want to live now that there's something to live for."

Linda came to the bed and James put his arm around her while his other hand still held her father's.

"God has been wonderful," James said through lips that trembled. "He kept me from finding you and becoming a murderer and He let me find love and happiness where hate and misery have been for so long. How glad I am that the search is ended! Now we can all spend our lives trying to make others as happy as we shall be."

"I thank Him that, unworthy as I am, He has forgiven

191

me and that he has given you the grace to forgive me also,'' Mr. Martinez murmured brokenly.

James turned to Linda as he held her close and said with a smile, ''With you in my arms and love filling my heart, I can truly say that this is a sweet revenge. And I do thank God for it.''

He bent and kissed her while her parents looked on with tears of happiness in their eyes and smiles on their lips.